CW01079780

BAKER & DAGGER INVESTIGATORS BOOK ONE

SAMANTHA PARRY

ISBN: 978-1-7916-1310-5

The Case of the Replacement Chef was first published in Local Magic: an
anthology of New Writing from Antimatter Press in 2015

Cover print courtesy of antiqueprints.com

DEDICATION

This book is dedicated to my parents, who have listened to me waffle on about characters, descriptions, theories, plots and missed deadlines for far too long.

CONTENTS

Acknowledgments   i

THE CASE OF THE REPLACEMENT CHEF

1   The Client   Pg 1
2   The Woman and Child   Pg 9
3   The Lord   Pg 17
4   The Chef   Pg 24

THE CASE OF THE WRONG TUNE

1   Terrance   Pg 33
2   The Organ Grinder   Pg 40
3   Mr Innocent and Colossus   Pg 47
4   The Bank   Pg 56

THE CASE OF TOO MANY FISH

1   The Accused   Pg 69
2   The Victim   Pg 78
3   The Partners   Pg 85
4   The Son   Pg 91

THE CASE OF THE WOLFPACK KILLERS

1   The Body   Pg 98
2   Clues   Pg 105
3   Another Early Morning   Pg 114
4   The Maze   Pg 120

THE TAKEOVER BID AFFAIR

1   Early Evening   Pg 129
2   Late Evening   Pg 137
3   The Early Hours   Pg 144
4   Dawn   Pg 154

ACKNOWLEDGMENTS

This collection exists because Sibylle Heidelberger pushed me into submitting a story to Antimatter Press for their first publication in 2015. Without her Polly and Will would not be where they are now.

Thank you to all the people that have helped me along the way with support and reading of my drafts. To name but a few of them:

Annet & David Portlock for believing their daughter can write.

Jenny Patrick who helps me believe in myself.

Liam O'Grady and Alexander Jonas for your insightful emails which gave me really useful feedback.

Tom and James Fackrell the brothers who I promise will arrive in prose at some point.

Mike Duran for the time you took to proof read my first final drafts and then go over them all again when I decided I was ready to publish.

THE CASE OF THE REPLACEMENT CHEF

1 THE CLIENT

"You'll never be getting those copper pans as bright as your 'air, Miss Polly, however much you polish 'em. And standing there staring out the window ain't going to bring the client you's so sure is coming any quicker, now is it?" Mr Hardaker said.

Polly turned to him. "No, I guess it isn't."

"Well then, why don't I get young Will to go and tidy up the display out front, then he can give you fair warning if he sees 'em coming, 'cause I need you to be working on the paperwork. As I 'ave been asking you to do for days, 'ave I not?"

"Yes, Mr Hardaker, you have, I'll do it now," she said. Lifting the stack of saucepans in front of her on the crowded shelf she placed the one she had been polishing underneath and replaced the stack. She lined up the handles, gave the stack one more swipe with her duster and stepped down from the wooden step ladder. Making her way back to the shop's counter she wove her way past the hat stands used to store pokers, stair rods, curtain poles and anything else of a certain length which wouldn't fit on a shelf or in a drawer. She pushed in a long thin drawer, which she knew Will would have left open in the tall chest of drawers which held every length of nail available, along with door handles, knobs and knockers, bolts, locks, studs, drawer handles, hinges, letter plates and blank decorative plates which could be engraved as desired. She had once promised that she would arrange everything in the chest of drawers into a workable arrangement. However, that promise had stood for so long that if she tried to change the order now, none of them would be able to find anything.

She made it to where Mr Hardaker stood behind the shop's countertop, his strong, battered hands on the wooden surface showing that in his earlier years he had plied his trade in a forge. They were pitted with burn spots where hot iron had managed to burn through his protective gloves, callouses merging with liver spots and wrinkled skin. A smile creased his face as he lifted the moveable part of the countertop to let her come through from the main store area.

"Thank you, Miss Polly, you know 'ow much I appreciate your 'elp with the books."

Polly smiled in return as she went past him and towards the office at the back of the store.

Mr Hardaker bellowed out for Will and she heard Will's deep affirmative reply and his strong footsteps sound on the stairs coming up from the cellar into the store.

She turned to survey the cluttered office and chuckled as Will's cry of pain and the ringing sound of pans, hung from the ceiling, clattering together reached her. It was amazing that someone who was normally so alert to the world around him could continually forget to duck on his way through the store. The bell above the front door rang and then the door shut on his cursing. She knew she could now concentrate on something else and let her mind stop obsessing about the client her instinct had told her would be arriving at some point during the day. Why her instinct couldn't be more specific as to an actual minute, hour or even whether something was going to happen in the morning or afternoon was a continual point of annoyance to her.

The office was small and even more cluttered than the shop. Shelving was attached to every wall space, large ledgers jostled for space alongside boxes full of receipts held down with iron balls or old horseshoes. Mr Hardaker's big office desk sat beneath the only window in the room; a small diamond paned aperture layered with dust and grime. It was so dirty that only a speck of light drifted through into the room heightening the shadows in the corners and the dust lying on every available surface. She looked at all the paperwork piled up on the desk and stuffed into the pigeon holes and sighed. "Who got the better deal in this working relationship?" she said to herself.

"Ah well, start at the beginning and somewhere along the line I will come to the end," she continued as she found a basket and began pushing the papers into it. Only when the desk was clear and the basket full did she sit down in the old leather swivel chair, pick up the first bit of paper from the basket and set it down on the desk before her.

Within a few minutes all thoughts of a new client had disappeared, and she was engrossed in invoices and orders. Neat piles of paper were growing on the desk and it was almost a shock to her when she reached down and realised the basket was empty. Collecting the big leather-bound ledger from the shelf next to the desk, she dutifully filled in details and filed the paperwork away in neat date-order bundles in the Gadget-made box files. As an added touch, she whispered a few simple words, flicked her fingers and the dust that had collected on the desk danced its way into the rubbish bin.

She went back out into the store and was just in the process of telling Mr Hardaker that all was done, when Will came running in.

"I reckon that client you was talking about this morning is outside. There's a woman out there Polly what 'as been past this shop six times in the last thirty minutes. I reckon she's plucking up the courage to see you."

"You go on up, Miss Polly, if'n she comes in I'll put 'er at ease and send 'er up to you, don't you worry now," Mr Hardaker assured her.

Polly smiled her thanks, ran up the worn carpeted stairs to the landing and opened the door to her and Will's office on the second floor. The door's upper half was frosted glass, adorned with the words "Baker & Dagger, Investigators," painted in neat black script.

In strong contrast to the shop and office below, this space was as neat as a pin. To the right of the entrance a wide desk stood in front of the only window, which was remarkably clean considering the filth that was inherent to the London air outside. Simple lace curtains hung down from a wrought iron curtain rail covering the whole window, ensuring privacy for the clients who ventured up the stairs. The midday sun shone through the lace and threw shadow patterns across the scuffed leather stretched across the top of the desk.

Along the wall opposite the door was a plain fireplace with two old leather armchairs arranged in front. A threadbare patterned rug covered the majority of the wooden floor and a vase of flowers stood on the mantelpiece. There were no other ornaments displayed. Polly had found over time that clients had trouble believing that a woman could be a detective and having pretty knick-knacks around only made it harder. So the office was neat and tidy, which she hoped reflected a professional ambiance to prospective clients.

The bell above the door rang; Polly knew that Mr Hardaker had pulled the lever down in the store warning her that her visitor would soon be with her. She quickly went into the small bathroom area at the back of the office to check in the mirror. She sighed at the sight of herself, with hair askew from running her hands through it doing Mr Hardaker's paperwork and a smudge of ink across her cheek. She wiped her face clean with a flannel, hastily pinned the escaped curls back into place and had just sat down behind her desk when a tentative knock sounded at the door.

"Please come in," she said, took a deep breath, relaxed and rose calmly from her chair to meet the prospective client.

The door opened to show a smart woman in plain dull-coloured walking clothes. Her crinoline was small in circumference and she had pushed back the hood of her cape and undone the ribbon holding it closed. Polly could see slight changes in the strength of colour near seam lines on her bodice and jacket; it had obviously been altered to accommodate an increase in weight as she got older. The one affectation was a stripe of purple through her grey hair which was swept back into a neat bun.

Polly went over to her, deciding immediately that the armchairs would be a better spot to converse than the official desk.

"Please, will you sit at the fireplace and tell me how I can help you? May I take your cape; I can hang it up for you whilst we talk."

The woman hesitated, looked back over her shoulder as if to turn and leave, then a thought flickered across her face and she nodded once, took off her cape, handed it to Polly and moved across to the right-hand chair. She sat down and clasped her hands neatly together on her lap. It was only a slight tug at the corner of her mouth where she caught her lip in her teeth that showed her nervousness.

Polly carefully hung her cape on the hook next to the door before turning to her.

"There is tea if you would like some," offered Polly.

"No, thank you," she said her voice soft and deep in tone.

Polly sat down in the chair opposite and smiled.

"Then how may I help you?"

The woman made to speak, stopped, considered, tried again but still no words came out.

"My name is Pollyanne Baker, what is yours?" asked Polly.

"I am … my name is Victoria … Victoria Pierce and I'm really not sure if you can help me, you see I'm not really sure anything is wrong but…"

"Why don't you just start at the beginning and tell me your concerns and then we can see what action we should take?"

"Very well," Miss Pierce hesitated a moment longer but then began.

"You see, Miss Baker, I am a woman of minor independent means and have never felt the desire to have a partner in my life. However," she hesitated, "however, a few months ago I met someone. He is an interesting man and has very quickly become important to me. The problem is that for the past few weeks he has seemed distracted and whilst he still says the right words, they sound wrong. I apologise, I am not explaining this well. It is just that if there is a hard truth to be faced, I want to know what it is — this not knowing is very distressing. So, as I am unable to get an answer from him, I am hoping that you can find the answer for me."

"Do you think there is another woman, then? Because you must understand, Miss Pierce that I am not in the business of tracking down unfaithful partners."

"Yes, I understand that and I realise this is may end up being very unseemly and a little sordid, but I am willing to pay you whatever you need to find out the truth. It may well be another woman, but it might also be something else entirely. He has always struck me as a responsible man; his recent actions have been against what I have learnt about him. Please help me. I am pretty certain that I am going to be hurt by whatever you tell me, but I cannot continue with things as they are."

Polly looked at the woman and was about to respectfully decline to take on the case when something tugged at her senses. She looked intently at Miss Pierce but all she saw was a normally confident woman out of her depth and vulnerable. She smiled softly and said, "I will do what I can, Miss Pierce. When are you next meeting this man?"

"This afternoon, Miss Baker, hence my visit to you now. I am on my way to meet him. We will be having afternoon tea in town."

"Then my associate and I will accompany you and follow this man when he takes his leave of you. I will take on your case as long as you are prepared for any news that I bring you in this regard. It is rare for a situation such as this to end happily."

"I know, Miss Baker. Men are often cruel and unthinking. But I have survived thus far and if the news is bad, I will not fall apart: I am a strong woman and will continue with my life. I need to know, whatever the outcome I am sure the truth will be better than this uncertainty."

Polly rose from her chair, helped Miss Pierce with her cape before collecting her own cape and bag from behind the desk and escorted Miss Pierce back down to the ground level.

"Where's Will, Mr Hardaker?" she asked.

"Out back, Miss Polly, working with young Gadget on some new fandangled thing the kid wanted to build. Did you want him?"

"Yes, please, if you could give him a call."

Mr Hardaker pulled a lever on the wall next to the desk. From a hook on the same wall he picked up a funnel attached to tubing and spoke into it.

"Will! Miss Polly needs you in the front, look sharpish and smarten yourself up before you come through."

"I shall be outside with Miss Pierce and attempting to hail a hansom cab. I doubt we will be back before closing time, Mr Hardaker."

"That's all right, Miss Polly, I can cope and shut up the store, I did it before you came and I can still do it now. Gadget will 'elp. Be off with you and I wish you success."

Polly had just managed to hail a cab when Will came out of the store. He was tugging his waistcoat into place and pulling a cap onto his head in an attempt to hide the fact that his long hair was refusing to stay neatly tied back. He opened the door of the cab and gallantly offered a hand to Miss

Pierce to assist her getting into the vehicle.

"Where are we going Miss Pierce?" asked Polly.

"Tell the driver we are headed for Paddington Station, there is Tea Room called Brunel's Tea Rooms nearby. If he knows it then warn him I will call for him to stop a little before we get there in order for you to disembark."

Polly went forward and looked up at the cabbie sat on his high seat holding the reins to his pair of strong chestnut matched pair of horses. He doffed his cap to her and smiled.

"It's alright Miss, I 'eard the lady, I know's where we're 'eaded. You hop in and I'll do me best to make it a smooth ride."

Polly went back and climbed up in the carriage; she settled in her seat and heard the cabbie call out to his horses. The cab lurched as the horses pulled the weight of them and then the wheels began to turn and they were on their way into town. The three occupants didn't attempt to talk as the dirty streets of London passed by. The cobblestones under the wheels rattled the cab so much any small talk would have been lost and dust coming ups from the streets to coat their clothes with a fine grey powder could also send an unwary person into a coughing fit. Thankfully the journey was short and soon Miss Pierce called for the cab to stop and let Polly and Will disembark.

Polly climbed out first, let Will go past her and then as she closed the door of the carriage she looked up at Miss Pierce.

"If you see us when you are with him, do not alert him to our presence. We will follow him when he leaves you. I doubt we will be able to tell you anything further today but will get word to you as soon as we know anything for certain," she promised.

"Thank you, Miss Baker; I appreciate your help in this matter." Miss Pierce called out to the cabbie, "Drive on, please, my good man", and the cabbie flicked his whip, the horses began to walk and the cab moved on and away. The two began to walk along the road following it. Will looked down at Polly, as he matched his long stride to her shorter one.

"Not another cheating man case, Polly! I thought we agreed we wouldn't take on any more of these cases: people are always being unfaithful to each other and we're the only ones that suffer on account we never get paid. Cause the offended party is either too 'eartbroken or too angry with us to part with the money they promised us."

"I know Will but something about it all bothered me and my instinct is suggesting there is something else here, not just a man being cruel. So humour me for a bit and we can always use it to improve our skills in following people."

"I don't need to improve my skill in that department and neither do you. Can't you just say a few words of your mumbo jumbo to him and get the truth? You done that before, why not now?"

"If something is wrong I don't think using my mumbo jumbo — as you so kindly call it — will give us the right answer. Employing my — what I call — brilliance at the beginning of a case could run the risk of telling us nothing whilst alerting someone to our interest before we are ready."

"You's the senior partner, Polly. Let's 'ope we don't get into too much danger, you know 'ow much I like a quiet life."

"You are such a liar sometimes, Will Dagger, you really are," she said, smiling up at him.

They turned the corner and saw Miss Pierce exiting the hansom cab in front of a smart tea shop near Hyde Park.

"May I have the pleasure of buying you a cup of tea, Polly?" asked Will, pushing out one elbow as an invitation.

She placed her hand on his arm and laughed. "Now that is the best suggestion you've had so far."

They walked across the cobblestone street to the tea shop and went inside.

The interior of the shop was laid out with a long serving counter to the right-hand side and small round tables filling up every available bit of space that remained. Polly saw Miss Pierce at a table at the back, so she steered Will to one nearer the front. Will went up to the counter to order tea and cake for them both.

He came back carrying a tray loaded with a china teapot, cups, saucers, milk jug and small plates holding rich fruit cake. As he placed them all on the table and sat down next to her, a gentleman came through the front door. He looked around and then went over to Miss Pierce, bending down to kiss her on the cheek and say a few words, before going to the counter to order where Polly got her first good look at him.

There was nothing much to say about him, grey-haired and going bald but with a neat goatee and military bearing. He was much shorter than Will but in contrast to her companion the gentleman's clothing was expensive and well cut, though she did notice the hem of his trouser was a little worn. So, expensive tastes without the income to support them, she thought.

At first glance there was nothing to tell her what had set her instincts buzzing when Miss Pierce spoke about him. He seemed a perfectly normal middle-to late-aged Londoner who had survived being in the military and found some employment on his return. That he had seen some action was obvious in the slight limp that showed in his walk.

She looked at Will.

"Anything strike you?"

Will wrinkled his nose, his head cocked to one side. Polly smiled. It was a look she recognised: he was on to something, her instincts had been right, there was more to this situation than met the eye.

"There is something, don't know quite what, smells almost right but something's off, it's niggling at me and I can't pick it up. Almost as though it isn't him but something he's been in contact with."

"In that case, we can do nothing until he leaves, so let us enjoy the tea and cake," she said, picking up the elegant white teapot and pouring out a cup for him. They sat at the pretty round table, munching on rich fruit cake, sipping hot tea out of fine bone china teacups and chatting about work in the store and the weather and anything else that occurred to them. To the elderly women at the next table, they looked like nothing more than a young couple starting out in the world and working hard to make something of themselves. Polly and Will smiled to each other as they listened to the women gossip.

"Though I don't much go for the fashion of the younger women these days, Ethel, far too much leather and metal for my tastes."

"I agree, Maud, this penchant for the industrial look is very aggressive. Why did people stop liking velvet and lace? So much more feminine."

"Ah, they are leaving!" Polly whispered as the gentleman and Miss Pierce stood up from their table. She turned away from their view and waited until the couple had passed her and exited the café before standing up and letting Will help her on with her cape and escort her out of the cafe to pursue the pair.

"But a very attractive couple, wouldn't you agree, Ethel?"

"Indeed, Maud."

The door shut behind Polly and Will.

Will chuckled softly.

"An attractive couple, us?" he said, grinning.

"Really, the way some people gossip and jump to conclusions, you would think they had nothing better to do."

"Should I go back in and put them right?"

"No, be sensible for once: just tell me you saw which way our money went?" She looked up and down the street, but the pair had disappeared.

2 THE WOMAN AND CHILD

"Tell me you know where they went, Will?"

He smiled down at her, "Oh ye of little faith, you know I never lose someone once I've got 'old of their scent! They went this way." He indicated towards the left and confidently began to walk along the road towards the turning to Hyde Park. Once they had turned left again, she saw the couple in the distance.

"Voila!" he said, pointing them out. "Perfect cover for us too, plenty of people out enjoying the sun."

There were indeed plenty of people, thought Polly. The sun had brought out the shoppers, the sight seers, the families, couples and those of ill repute. All levels of society mixing together as they walked along the pavements, jostling to stay on track at times. Wives nudged their husband's attention away from the lewd suggestions spoken by the women leaning against door frames and sitting on door steps. Children ran around, dodging between people before dashing back to the safety of their parents. Will, laughing bumped into a young boy, apologised, let the boy run on then showed Polly the fat wallet he had picked out of the boy's pocket. Then before Polly could say anything he had bumped into a portly gentleman, apologised profusely, brushed the man down, replaced the wallet into his coat and finished off by doffing his cap to the man before walking on.

"Can't let 'em win all the time, Polly" he said.

"You could have just given him his wallet back, instead of having to bump into him."

"I like practicing putting something back into a person's pocket as well as practicing taking something out."

"Can we keep in mind that we are supposed to be following our client and her beau and not calling attention to ourselves?"

"Don't worry Polly, I've got a 'old on them, we won't lose them.

They're a good way in front of us, they isn't seeing us."

They continued along the street, merging with the crowds and Will kept them on the right track, and within a short time they reached the edge of Hyde Park. Polly watched as the gentleman hailed a hansom cab, assisted Miss Pierce into it, kissed her cheek, spoke to the cabbie and then waved her off.

"Time to find out what his secret is," Polly said.

The man stood watching the hansom cab until it turned a corner and was out of sight and then he walked across the road and into the park. He did not look back and seemed oblivious now to anything around him. His pace increased and he walked without taking in any of the sights of the park.

They followed him and watched as he approached a bench alongside the central lake known as the Serpentine for the way it curved like a snake. The man sat down and stared straight ahead, heedless of the sights in front of him. People were out boating on the lake and an ice-cream seller was enticing buyers with wondrous descriptions of the flavors he had available.

Finding a space near a large tree just uphill from the bench, Polly and Will settled down to see what happened next, blending in with the many other park-goers sitting on blankets and enjoying the late afternoon autumn sun.

"How annoying," moaned Polly as she saw the gentleman rise to his feet and bow as a woman and small child arrive. He kissed her cheek and indicated for them to both sit down. "It had to be. Bother! I thought it would be something else."

"It is something else," frowned Will.

"What do you mean? Look, he's fooling around with another woman, age-old story. I'm going to have to go and tell Miss Pierce the sad fact that the man she has fallen for has another woman on the side and she has a child, quite possibly his."

"Yes, that is what it looks like… but that woman and child, they're not human."

Polly looked at him.

"Are you sure?"

"They don't smell right; they're missing the base notes of scent that I associate with all humans. They don't smell of anything I 'ave come up against before but it's the same scent what I picked up on him in the café."

"*That* I picked up, not *what*," Polly reprimanded automatically before adding, "What on earth have we stumbled upon?"

"Lord knows what," Will replied, "though I suppose the Lord would know that as well. Guess we'll just 'ave to wait and see."

The three people sitting at the bench finally rose as the sun began to go down and everyone around them began packing up their belongings and leaving the park. With a kiss on the cheek as goodbye, the man left the pair and walked toward the exit without looking back. The woman and child remained at the bench.

"Which do you want to follow?" Polly asked.

"I'll stay with the woman and child, easier for me to slip into wolf 'ere if necessary, a 'uman in the park late will be noticed. I might get away with being thought nothing more than a large dog."

"Be careful and we will meet back at the office once each side is settled for the evening, wherever that might be."

She blew him a kiss as she walked away and he continued to watch her for a while. Her skills at remaining unnoticed were exceptional considering her style of dress and appearance.

The evening sun was catching the highlights in her rich red hair that tumbled in curls down her back. The dark burgundy leather corset she wore had clever additions that held picklocks and small weapons that on casual inspection would seem nothing more than elaborate decoration.

That she had little need of them was a continual source of amusement for Will. With her power, she could make a door fly off its hinges or coax it to open but most times she would happily employ her skills as a sneak thief rather than speak spells.

"And she thinks you're all right, my old son, so don't disappoint 'er, keep your mind on the job."

He looked back to the bench where the woman and child had been, only to find it empty.

"Bleeding 'ell, where 'ave you two got to now?" he swore as he looked around. He caught their scent just as he glimpsed them heading farther along the banks of the Serpentine. He hurried after them, all the while trying to look as nonchalant as possible. "That'll learn you for day-dreaming," he murmured as he finally caught up with the pair and could slow down and keep pace with them. If he didn't know better, he thought to himself, the pair looked perfectly normal, the kid bouncing along, skipping whilst keeping a tight hold of the woman's hand and she was chatting away to him as she pointed out the swans gliding over the lake.

Then they abruptly stopped at the stone bridge that spanned the lake and all pretense of happy normality dropped away. Will was glad that he had instinctively remained out of their sight and was now concealed behind a large tree. Instead of risking exposing himself to their sight, he used his acute senses of smell and hearing to stay informed of their movements as they stood at the water's edge. He guessed they were probably taking the time to ensure that they were not being watched.

Then Will heard a splash and curiosity got the better of him. He considered looking round the trunk of the tree but instead looked up and with one jump reached up to the lowest branch some two feet above him and pulled himself into the concealing foliage. He looked out through the leaves just in time to see the pair disappear through an opening in the stonework supporting the bridge on the other side of the lake. Then they were gone and the stonework was back as it always was, leaving no clue that there was an entrance there at all. He stared at it in amazement. "Blimey if I hadn't seen that I would never 'ad believed someone's telling of it" he thought.

Jumping back down, Will walked over to the water's edge and looked across at the stonework. How on earth had they got across the lake in the time it took him to climb the tree, it had only a matter of seconds between hearing the splash and seeing them enter the bridge. He sniffed the air and the faint scent of the woman and child told him they went straight across the water.

Tentatively he went to take a step into the water to follow them but as he did so the strongest feeling hit him that he oughtn't. He stepped back and the feeling disappeared. Curious, he moved a little nearer to the bridge, tried again and the same feeling assaulted his senses. He walked up and onto the bridge and tried a few times to climb over it to drop down into the lake but each time the strange inhibition came over him.

Crossing over the bridge, he walked along the other side of the lake for a few yards and then went to step in. Nothing happened, except of course the feeling of the water filling his boots and his feet sinking into the mud. "Lovely," he thought sourly. Staying close to the water's edge and carefully placing each foot as he didn't want to find himself sinking any further than his calves, he made his way toward the bridge. When he was about twenty yards away the feeling hit him again.

He sighed, turned and walked back through the mud and climbed back out onto the pathway. Whatever it was that was happening, it was protected by some pretty powerful magic. His and Polly's instincts were correct: something was wrong and something would have to be done about it.

Though, he thought to himself, there was little he could do now. Odds were that the pair had retired for the evening. So unless he wanted to sit there as the night grew dark and cold, with boots saturated with water and mud, he would be much better suited to heading back to the office. Then he could find out how Polly had fared following the gentleman and they could decide together on the next course of action.

"She'll want you to come up with something though, won't she? Can't go back with nothing, can't let her think of everything. Partners is what we are and partners share the load. So, how to get across a barrier designed to deter a 'uman being?"

Will sat watching the lake and area around the bridge for a while and then a smile crept onto his face.

"Now that might work," he thought and without another look he made his way along to the path leading out of the park and started to run. It wasn't the most comfortable thing to do but at least people wouldn't have much time to hear his feet squelching and wonder what he had been doing.

He kept up a sensible pace so that no Peelers out on the beat would think he was up to anything nefarious and was rather just late for a meeting with a girl or friends. At times, due to the sheer number of people out and about, he had to slow down and walk but soon he got past the centre of town and made his way to the back streets and the routes that normal, sensible people wouldn't choose. Though if anybody tried to accost him, they would find out very quickly that he had claws.

Thankfully, Will got back to the shop with no delays and using his key, he sped upstairs so he could peel off his boots and wet socks. He considered lighting a fire but was pretty certain that once Polly returned and they talked through what he had seen they would be back out the door and visiting the Serpentine to investigate further. So he just went up to his room above the office, changed his trousers, laid the wet ones across his chair to dry out and found clean socks and his second pair of boots.

He had just finished pushing old newspapers into his boots to help them dry out when he heard someone come in the back door. His nose told him it was Polly, so he set the wet boots next to his chair and went down the stairs to greet her.

"I've sommat strange to tell you about the woman and child. What about the man?"

Polly went over to the desk and hoisted herself up to sit on it, with her legs dangling down and showing off her neat laced boots.

"Not a thing. I followed him back to his lodgings in Camden. He went in and up to his room and as far as I could make out he settled down for the night. Certainly he drew the curtains and within ten minutes the light went down to a single lamp. I went into the building and investigated: he rents one room in the whole house. It is not the most expensive accommodation but clean and tidy. I spoke to the landlady. Ensured that she won't remember me asking anything, just in case the man enquires. She told me he was well-spoken, never gave her any trouble and up to a few weeks ago she used to have daily chats with him. Now he comes back to the house, goes straight up to his room with hardly a word to her and locks his door."

"Something's 'appened to him then, that's two people who've reported a change in 'is character. Shall I tell you what I found out?"

"Yes, please."

Will related his experience and watched as Polly listened, occasionally asking him to elaborate on something, her feet swinging back and forth as she pondered the situation.

"So the barrier around the bridge… would anyone getting near it be as aware of it as you were?"

"I thought about that. I was doing me best to get across, so the feeling might 'ave been stronger but to anyone walking along the path it would just be a simple nudge to keep going."

"We need to go back and see if we can get past it. Any ideas?"

"One but I'd like to give it a go before I tell you what it is."

Polly jumped down from the desk.

"Right then, I'll just change into more appropriate clothing and we'll get moving."

She disappeared to her room upstairs and soon emerged in knee-high, low-heeled boots, dark trousers and shirt and a long jacket that showed numerous odd bulges in different-sized pockets all over it.

"Ready?" she asked.

Will nodded and they left the office and walked down the stairs and out. Hailing a cab, they moved quickly through the town and were soon back at Hyde Park.

"The expenses are beginning to pile up," said Polly, "I hope our Miss Pierce is good for them."

"Doubtful, when we tell 'er about the other woman and child," commented Will dryly.

"'Twas ever thus with this sort of case," Polly replied ruefully.

They walked down through the park to the bridge. Polly tried to step into the lake and immediately stepped back.

"Wow!" she exclaimed, startled. "That's a powerful deterrent, very clever as well, nobody would notice it but just have a feeling that they oughtn't step into the lake. But there are signs everywhere that you shouldn't, so no-one would think anything of their seemingly singular decision not to go in there. So how do you propose we get past it?"

"It may be a deterrent against curious humans but look at the swans, ducks and the other birds; they ain't bothered and I bet if we looked we'd see at least one water rat not worrying about it neither. So I'm thinking if I changed then I would 'ave no problems in walking through it."

"And me?" asked Polly.

"Ever thought of being a rat? I could carry you over then."

"I'd prefer to be a cat; rats are not exactly clean."

"Very well, just don't be a fat cat."

"As if I would be! I shall ensure I'm nothing less than a beautiful ginger pedigree."

"Are there such things? And aren't all ginger cats toms?"

"Shut up and change, so we can try out your theory. If we stand here like this for much longer people will start to be curious about us. Come on, we'll head up the bank and find a place to hide your clothes."

They walked up to the tree Will had climbed before and Polly kept watch to ensure no-one would appear and be able to see what he was about to do. Will stripped naked, wrapped his clothes up into a ball and hid them in the shrubbery next to the tree. Then he crouched down and allowed his mind to relax into his other form. Slowly his back elongated and as he stretched, his arms lengthened and his legs shortened. Then his head shook, his body followed suit and the change took hold as fur rippled along his naked skin. He groaned with pleasure as his senses became more aware of the smells and sounds of the night around him. The grass had caught the scent of evening, warm under his paws from the afternoon. The scratching of a squirrel made him pause, it would make a nice snack but then the clean flowery scent of Polly brought him back to the evening's task.

He gave a soft chuff and pushed his nose into Polly's hand, making her jump.

"Why do you have to do that? You know I hate your wet nose, it's all cold and slippery, you horrible wolf."

Will cocked his head to one side and Polly could almost swear he was laughing at her. He sat back on his haunches and looked expectantly at her.

"Oh no, I'm not doing anything until you've proved your theory. So go on, try and get through the barrier."

Will gave a small growl of annoyance and then carefully walked up to the edge of the lake and took a tentative step into the dark water, then another, until he stood with all four paws immersed. He turned to look back at Polly.

"Clever wolf. Very well, I shall soon be on your back. Do not let me fall in, I do not wish to find myself swimming and you know how much cats hate water, so beware my claws."

She looked up at the night sky, held out her hands and began to speak:

"In this dark night let my eyes see clear,
To find the truth a feline I appear.
With the strength of the earth I set my charm.
So let it be and none may it harm."

Her hands dropped to her sides, she crouched down, blinked and her eyes opened to a different world. She could smell the same squirrel that had interested Will. As she took a step forward, her body moved in a different way. She shook herself once and then walked elegantly down to the lake, nimbly jumped up onto Will's back and settled herself down on his soft fur. He turned his head back to look at her and she batted his ear with her paw. He gave a small bark, looked forward again and began to make his way across the lake. He had expected the water to get deep enough that he would have to swim but a concealed walkway just below the surface made it easy to cross. In fact the water never came high enough to reach his body and it was a simple task to get to the solid patch of earth next to the stonework that supported the bridge on the other side of the lake.

Polly jumped down and reversed her spell. She stood up next to Will and rested her hand on his head. She ruffled his fur affectionately.

"Good thinking, Will, now let's see how we get into the hidden lair."

She reached into one of the numerous pockets on her jacket and pulled out a small opaque circle set in a metal casing. She flicked a switch at the back so that a gentle light appeared. Stepping up to the stonework, she shined her lamp on it and inspected it carefully.

"Ah, a lock with a push-button, so some have keys and some are given entrance. Hmm, I doubt anyone would let us in if we pushed the bell but let's see if Gadget's new toy will work on the lock."

A reach into another pocket brought out a very short thin metal tube, with thinner metal rods hanging from it attached by minute springs. At the other end was a small handle that Polly now turned. Placing it into the lock until it stopped, she turned it to engage and then let go of the handle. Each rod reacted and lengthened or shortened as required and it clicked into place. She turned it a little more to engage and the door opened. She pulled the key out, locked it to retain the shape and put it back into her pocket.

"Perfect, clever Gadget! Come on, Will, my wolf, let's see what is hidden from view underneath the Serpentine."

3 THE LORD

Polly raised the lamp to illuminate the dark corridor in front of them. As they walked along, the corridor sloped down, until they reached an open area that branched into two corridors opposite them.

"Which way, I wonder?" Polly queried.

Will padded over and sniffed the air at each opening. Looking at Polly, he moved back toward the right-hand corridor.

"We can go that way if you think it will prove interesting. Any specific reason?"

Will stepped up to her, sniffed her and wagged his tail, then went back to the right-hand corridor, sunk low to the ground and gave a low growl.

"That way smells of the woman and child?"

Will stood back up, looked at her, wagged his tail again and began to walk down the corridor.

"Fine, we'll go and see what's down the hole then," said Polly. She followed him, raising the lamp to light the way forward.

The corridor continued downward in a right-hand circular direction, leading them back on themselves until they reached a plain wooden door. Polly was pretty certain that they had moved back under the Serpentine. She gently tried the door handle. Finding that it wasn't locked, she pushed, hoping no-one was behind it but only silence greeted the pair.

Polly turned a knob at the back of the lamp and the light grew stronger, illuminating a large room. Directly in front of them hung a coffin-style container, one of many suspended from the ceiling. Looking up, Polly could see that the container was attached to a track system, so that it could be pulled along and moved. The containers went around the room in a circle, two deep with a central open space. She figured that containers could be pulled into the middle ring and then directed somewhere else. She looked through the gaps between the containers and saw that, opposite to where she and Will stood; there was an opening out into another corridor.

She stepped up to the container in front of them and realised she was at its back. Moving round to the front, she saw a push-button panel on the right-hand side that would require entering a code to open it up. Putting the lamp down on the ground, she went again into a pocket, this time pulling out a small pot and brush. Twisting the lid off the pot, she dipped the brush into the powder inside and then swept it across the panel. She tapped the loose powder back into the pot and replaced the lid; both disappeared back into her pocket. Picking up the lamp, she looked again at the panel and saw that the powder had settled where someone had pressed certain numbers. Considering that most people would start from the top and work down, Polly pressed the appropriate buttons. There was a click and the container door opened slightly. She took hold and opened it more fully.

"Well, that I did not expect," she whispered, as she looked into the container.

Inside was a woman dressed in normal everyday clothing. Servant's clothing, Polly thought to herself, no crinoline or corset, just simple work clothes. Her face was older, with crow lines around her shut eyes. To all intents and purposes, she appeared to be asleep. Though the tubing that snaked up from a large glass bottle at the base of the container and then entered into the woman's neck was highly suspicious.

"Very odd," muttered Polly.

Will stepped closer and sniffed at the figure, then shook his head and growled.

As the woman didn't stir, Polly began to examine her closely. Nothing seemed out of place, other than the obvious fact that there was a servant woman inside a container in a dark chamber under Hyde Park. Polly lifted the cuff of the woman's shirt and saw a faint dark line around her wrist, slightly raised as though it were scar tissue. Polly touched it and then picked at it until her nail caught under it and she felt the skin give. She carefully pulled the skin away and rolled it up the woman's arm.

"Even odder," she murmured.

Underneath the skin was a collection of metal rods and cables, simulating the bones, muscles and veins that would be found in a human arm.

"It's a robot, a humanoid robot! What is going on down here?" she exclaimed, looking down into Will's bicoloured eyes. He pushed up against her and rubbed his muzzle against her hand in agreed amazement.

"Shall we continue or leave now?" she asked as she rolled the skin back down and shut the container door. Will moved round the containers toward the opening into the far corridor in answer.

"Very well, farther in but carefully, as we don't want to alert anyone to our presence. I would like to sleep in my own bed tonight and not at the bottom of the lake."

They moved quietly round until they got to the opening and looked out.

With a glance at the corridor ceiling, Polly saw that the track led down to the right. Will was about to follow it when they both heard voices coming from within the corridor. She looked back but there was nowhere to hide amongst the containers.

A little way down the corridor on the opposite side from where they were standing was another door. Quickly, Polly walked down to it and tried the handle. The door opened and they both slipped inside. She pulled it closed behind them, hoping that whoever was coming wanted a container in the main chamber.

Heavy footsteps came closer and Polly heard two male voices, though through the closed door it was impossible to make out any words. She held her breath as they came alongside the door readying a power spell in her head but the voices faded as they continued into the container room. Soon she heard the sound of wheels running along the track, then the voices again as the men came back into the corridor, obviously pulling one of the containers along with them and down the corridor and away. Polly went to open the door but a soft yelp from Will made her turn back. He was standing next to a large desk that took up the better part of one side of the room.

"What is it, Will?" Polly asked as she went over to him.

She followed his gaze and saw what he was looking at. A family crest was painted on the wall above the desk. Something about it registered in her mind but she couldn't catch hold of whose it was. Then notebooks on the desk caught her eye and she picked up the top one and opened it. Sets of letters and what looked like dates were written down one side and numbers down the other; it looked like the accounts she kept for Mr Hardaker but this made no sense to her. Whomever had made the notations was using a code known only to themselves.

"I think we need to find out what happens with the containers and then get out of here, don't you?" she whispered to Will, who wagged his tail in approval.

Together they went back out into the corridor and followed the direction the two men had taken. It wasn't long before they saw a bright light appear ahead of them and they crept closer, hugging the wall. They stopped as the corridor finished and an entrance appeared which showed iron steps leading downward as the track turned and disappeared from view. Polly and Will stepped close to the opening and looked round the wall and down to where, below them, the container was already attached to the floor and the door had been opened and removed, revealing a young man. Was this another humanoid robot, Polly wondered?

In the centre of the room was a massive black machine covered in dials and levers. It must be a robot, Polly realised, as she saw a thin tube looping down from the machine that then ran along the ground and up into the back of the open container, where it was inserted into the robot's neck. A tall, elegant man came half into view from behind the machine, his back toward Polly and she watched as his long well-manicured hand stroked the robot's cheek.

"So! Let us bring you back to life, my young man! You will fulfill your purpose, becoming part of my entourage to ensure I regain my rightful standing within this corrupt society that has stolen so much from me."

He reached over to the machine and pulled down a lever. There was a spark and the tubing began to ripple. Some sort of liquid was running through it and into the robot. Polly didn't want to hazard a guess what the fluid was.

The elegant man watched, then moved another dial and the tubing increased its movement. Abruptly he pulled the lever back up, went over to the back of the container and removed the tubing. He then returned to the front, unhooked what looked like a long-handled tuning fork from the machine and placed it close to the robot's heart.

"Now this might make you jump a little," he warned and touched it to the robot's body. With a jolt its whole body jerked and shuddered, then the eyes sprang open and a cry of pain echoed around the room.

"Welcome back!" the man exclaimed as the robot collapsed, gasping, to the floor. The man crouched down to help the robot back up to standing and Polly nearly cried out as she saw the elegant face: she recognised him! The man stopped moving, raising his head to look in her direction. Polly immediately backed away from the entrance and turned to Will, motioning that they needed to get out fast.

The two of them ran up the corridor, through the container room and back up to the main entrance. Polly pulled out the key she had created earlier. It fit smoothly into place and they were outside in minutes.

Will stood ready as he felt the shimmer of power ripple through the air and then the ginger cat landed on his back. He ran across the lake and up behind the tree, where he changed back into human form and bent down to find his clothes.

"You haven't got time for that, can you get us both up into the tree, now?" she breathed, already changed to human as quickly as before.

Will looked at her curiously but bent down and joined his hands together so that she could place one foot in them. He hoisted her upward and she caught hold of the lowest branch and pulled herself up. Will joined her and they both climbed a little farther up into the concealing foliage. They froze in place as, through a gap in the leaves, they saw a heavyset man appear at the stone entrance. He stood there swinging a lamp around in a slow arc, searching the area. The light swung across the tree but thankfully he never raised it up any higher than ground level, which might have illuminated the hidden pair.

"There's no-one 'ere," he called over his shoulder. "The barrier is in place, no-one could have got through it, 'is Lordship must have been 'earing things."

A voice replied but Polly and Will couldn't hear what was said. The man sent the light in one more arc, then shrugged, turned and went back inside the bridge. Silence descended.

"Can we get down? It's bloody freezing and I've got branches trying to get into places they aren't supposed to go!" grumbled Will quietly.

"Wait for a bit," whispered Polly. "They might think to come back out and check again."

"It's all right for you, you get to keep your clothes on during a change. I have to take mine off, otherwise they're ripped to shreds."

"Stop fussing, you're supposed to be a vicious hot-blooded wolf, a bit of cold won't kill you."

"Well don't mind me feeling just a tad exposed. Being naked as a new-born babe sitting up a tree with a witch isn't normal behaviour."

Polly grinned. "Which bit isn't normal, being naked in a tree or being so with a witch? Would it be normal if I wasn't a witch?"

"Now you're confusing the issue, just like you always did when we got caught out at the orphanage."

"Got us out of trouble, didn't it?"

"About as often as it got us into trouble," he said. "Come on, let's get down, they ain't coming back out."

"All right, you go first, you can catch me if I fall."

Will jumped down, pulled his clothing out from its hiding place as Polly made her way down to the lowest branch. Without warning him she took hold, swung herself down and let go. Dropping his clothes and spinning back, Will caught her just in time.

"You could have waited, let me get my trousers on at least", he grumbled.

"Why?"

"I'm naked, remember."

"Yes and I've seen you that way lots of times before, right from the time you came to me shivering after your first change. And anyway, what's the difference between you being naked up the tree with me compared to standing naked next to me on the ground?"

"Nothing, only it ain't seemly for a girl to be in the arms of a naked man! What would people think?"

"Look, there's hundreds of people around us at the moment, all of them sniffing down their noses at us. Oh, that old woman over there is having a good look at you, shame you're all cold and shriveled."

"Polly!"

She punched him lightly on the arm and said, "Put me down and stop being ridiculous, Will. Get dressed and let's get back, we have some thinking to do."

Will let her out of his arms and she turned away from him to look at the bridge and the concealed doorway.

"Hmm, indeed, I want to know what happened in there. What did you see?" asked Will as he began to get dressed.

"Let's get away first, just in case His Lordship decides to send them back out for a further look. I'll explain when we get back with a fire lit and a glass of something strong in our hands. That was a little too close for comfort. I don't think they would have locked us in a cupboard for a few hours as punishment for a transgression. Their solution would have been a more permanent one."

Will put his cap on his head and they made their way back to the main road, hailing a cab which took them quickly back to the office.

"So what is going on?" asked Will as he bent over the fire and coaxed a flame to the paper and kindling.

"Didn't you recognise the man?"

"No, I was looking at the robot. What the 'ell did he do to it?"

"I think he was bringing it to life. I know that sounds incredible," she continued, seeing Will's expression. "As to who the man is, I believe he is Lord Astborough but why he was animating an extremely lifelike robot is something that we need to discover and fast."

"Lord Astborough… I thought that name and family had disappeared into ignominy after that debacle on the stock exchange?"

"The father had; the son has recently returned to the fray and has been moving amongst the upper echelons of society. From the servant gossip I've listened into, there are some very high society ladies — I shall not name them — who find him irresistible and incredibly charming. On the other hand, the men do not hold him in the same regard but nothing has been vocalised in public against him."

"But what on earth 'as a lord coming back into society via the beds of ladies got to do with robots and a 'idden lair under the Serpentine in 'yde Park?"

"A good question but I don't think we will be able to find the answer tonight and I'm wary of going back to that place so soon after nearly getting caught out. We need to find another way to discover what he is planning."

She went into the kitchen and came back with two glasses and a bottle of brandy. Pouring a good measure in each glass, she passed one to Will and they sat down in the two armchairs. A comfortable silence descended as they both pondered the situation. A habit learnt in childhood, time for their own talent to draw conclusions, which together they could explore.

"What if…" began Will as Polly said "Perhaps…."

She smiled and said, "Go on, you first, I think it's your turn."

"Well, this is my thinking: whatever is going on, the man our client has asked us to follow is mixed up in it, whether by choice or not. So maybe if we follow 'im tomorrow morning and find out where he works and what he does, we might discover why Lord Astborough is interested in him. It might give us an inkling of what he is up to."

"My thoughts exactly. I don't really fancy an early start but I've a feeling we will need to be there at the crack of dawn so that we don't miss him leaving his home. Whatever else he is, he's ex-military and they are early risers."

4 THE CHEF

Dawn found them standing on a street corner that gave them a view of the gentleman's lodgings.

They breathed a collective sigh of relief as they watched him come smartly down the front steps and turn away from them with no inclination that he was worried anyone would be watching. He walked swiftly through the streets, tailed by Polly and Will, until he arrived at the gates of a very fine town house. He entered the gates, made his way round to the back of the building and disappeared from view. The investigators walked on a little and then Polly stopped and looked back.

"So that's where 'e works. Do we follow 'im in?" Will mused as he looked at Polly. "Now what?" he asked as he realised Polly wasn't looking at him but rather was staring back at the gates in astonishment.

"What is it?" he asked.

"Look, isn't that the young man from last night, the robot that was brought to life?" she asked, pointing.

Will looked and saw a young man go into the same gates, walk round the side of the house and disappear from view, just as the gentleman had done.

"Well, that's a coincidence!" he said. "What do we do now? It's 'ardly as if we can go up to the front door and say, 'Excuse me but did you know a 'ighly sophisticated robot has just walked into your servants' entrance?' We'd be carted off to Bedlam quicker than you could say Jack Robinson."

"Bother!" remarked Polly. "I know what is happening. It's nothing more than an elaborate case of blackmail. I bet you anything you like that the robot is collecting information for Lord Astborough to use against the owner of that house. How boring and mundane."

"Maybe but that's a pretty posh 'ouse. Whose is that crest over the gate?" Will asked.

Polly looked back at the gate and gasped.

"You're right, Will, I know that crest, it's the Prime Minister's. This must be his town house. If Lord Astborough is putting a robot into the Prime Minister's house, he might be planning something a little more destructive. He could be plotting to overthrow the government."

"But why didn't anyone notice that the young lad is now a robot? And aiming to attack the Prime Minster wouldn't bring down the government, would it?"

"It can't just be happening here, Will. Think about it. There were lots of containers in that room and maybe that wasn't the only room full of them. We didn't get the chance to search any further. If he has managed to get robots employed in important houses or offices all over the city, just think what damage he could do to the infrastructure of this country."

"But, Polly, what has the man we've been following got to do with all this? 'e isn't a robot, is he?"

"I rather think our client might have noticed and mentioned it if he had been. Come on, we need to go in and find out more. We might have just joined this plot at the best time to thwart it."

"Are we going to have to pretend to be collecting for a charity or some such, or...?"

"No, we need information and fast: I shall turn on my charm."

With that, Polly went back and through the gates, walking at a quick pace round to the servants' entrance. Will hurried to catch her up, hearing the words of the charm spell she was saying as she walked along. He had just pulled down his jacket to look smarter as the door was opened by a very austere butler, who looked down his nose at them with a very unfriendly face.

"I saw you come in the gates. Leave now, or I will have you thrown out."

Polly smiled, finished the spell, waved her hand, the air rippled and the man's face relaxed. He smiled back at her.

"Yes, my dear, how can I help you?"

"It's like this: we need to know about the two men that have come to work this morning, especially the young man who was here just before us."

"Oh, you mean young Benjamin."

"Do I? I suppose I do. Has he worked here long? Has he changed his habits or demeanour recently?"

"Funny you should mention that, my dear and might I say how beautiful you look on this glorious morning," the butler offered with a dreamy smile.

"Benjamin?" Polly reminded him.

"Oh yes, of course, so sorry. Now, he's worked here for, let me think now, yes, nearly three years and always been the chattiest of young men but within the last month or so, now that you've brought my attention to it, he's become much quieter of late and this morning I didn't get a single word out of him."

"And the older gentleman, that came in before him, with the goatee and military bearing?"

"Oh, that would be Chef. Now that is odd, you asking about Benjamin. I hadn't put the two things together, not at all, what with them working at different levels, you understand, now how did I miss that?"

The man looked at Polly.

"You are very beautiful, my lady, would you consider… maybe…?"

"What about Chef?" Polly asked.

"Ah well, come to think of it, Chef has gone the same way, he used to be happy to talk and would take the younger maids under his wing and look after them but now he has become most private. Oh my good Lord, is this something that should concern the Prime Minister? Should I be calling a Constable here and have the two arrested?"

"Oh no," said Polly. "It's nothing of any consequence. What time will Chef be finishing today?"

"He is actually leaving after lunchtime. My employer is eating out this evening so had no use for him."

"We will catch up with Chef later, then. Thank you for your help. I would, though, subtly keep Benjamin away from your employer's office."

"For one as beautiful as you, my lady, it would be a pleasure to perform any task you desire," he simpered as he continued to stand at the open doorway staring at Polly.

"Thank you. Do you not have duties to carry out?"

"Duties, my lady?"

"Yes, duties, off you go, shut the door, go about your business." She made a shooing motion with her hands.

"Oh, yes, of course. Well, goodbye then, my lady."

Polly and Will walked away, leaving the butler still standing in the doorway.

"Tell me your spell will wear off," Will mumbled.

"Yes, he'll be fine in about five minutes. Won't remember a thing, except of course the decision to keep Benjamin away from the Prime Minister."

"You're scary sometimes, Polly, you really are. What now?"

"We have a choice, Will: we either stand here until after lunch and then follow Chef, or we go back to the office, collect a few things and go straight to Hyde Park. I have a very strong feeling that we will see him there today."

"Park it is, then," he agreed.

###

26

"What time do you think they would have finished lunch? We couldn't be wrong, could we?" sighed Polly after they had been sitting for a few hours behind the same tree they had used the night before.

"No, 'ere they come now," said Will and Polly saw the woman, child and Chef coming along the path. This time the woman didn't hesitate or look around, she simply guided the man across the concealed walkway in the lake to the bridge and the stone door opened as they got to it. They walked swiftly inside and the door shut immediately.

"We give them a few minutes to move away from the main corridor and then we follow. Is it clear enough for us to change, or should I throw a cover spell?" asked Polly.

"No-one within seeing distance. I can smell a few near the other end of the lake but that is all."

"Then we enter the lion's den once more. Let us hope we get out again."

Will changed as Polly put his clothes in a bag, which she then tied around his neck before changing into the cat and taking her place on his back. Will made his way across the lake, resumed his human form and got dressed as Polly once more opened the hidden door with Gadget's key.

"Ready?" she whispered.

"At your back as always."

She smiled and stepped inside. Using the dim light from her lamp she began to retrace their steps of the night before but when they came to the choice of corridors, Polly indicated the left-hand corridor and looked at Will.

"We know where the right-hand corridor leads, shall we try the other one?" she whispered.

He smiled in agreement and Polly turned slightly to walk down the dark left-hand corridor.

The lamp showed them the way as the corridor curved on downward, until light showed up ahead and Polly turned it off. They crept forward until the corridor opened out onto a balcony that looked down onto the same room they had seen the night before; though this time they were on its opposite side. To their left at the end of the balcony, a circular staircase led down to the room's floor. Bright lights illuminated the other side of the room, throwing shadows over the balcony, allowing them to step closer to the edge and still remain partially hidden.

Looking directly across, they could see where they had hidden the night before at the point where the iron steps had begun. From this side of the room they could see the layout more clearly. Alongside the steps was a space large enough to hold a metal table that had a black cloth flung over it covering a lumpy shape. Along the wall behind the cloth-covered table were shelves stacked with glass jars, some empty, some full of different-coloured liquids, others half full and still more with odd solid shapes suspended in liquid.

"Some of those jars look like they're full of pickled gherkins, what on earth 'as he been doing?" Will whispered.

"It's the black arts, Will; he's been playing with the very essence of life itself. We have to stop him."

Polly took a step forward but Will held her back as Lord Astborough stepped into view.

"Wait a minute; we don't want to go down there until we know where everyone is. What about the two men from last night?"

They watched as Lord Astborough took hold of the cloth and pulled it away to reveal Chef on the table, held in place by metal cuffs across his legs, arms, body and neck. Lord Astborough offered a slim glass of what looked like champagne to Chef but got no reaction, other than a flick of his eyes.

"Do you think he's drugged?" whispered Will.

"He must be; I can hardly think he climbed onto that table willingly."

Their attention was drawn back to the lord as he spoke.

"You are the last piece, my dear man," he said. "Once you have been allowed to fulfill your potential, the balance of power in this city will topple and only one man will have the strength of character to step forward. What you do tomorrow will alter my fortune forever. But I jump ahead of myself: it is time to change your very self, it is time you met someone that you know very well."

Lord Astborough went to the wall and pressed a button. There was silence for a while but soon they heard the sound of a container being pulled along the track and the voices of two men. They came into view, stopped at the top of the room in order to send the container over the edge, before walking down the stairs and waiting for a command. The container continued running along the track down to ground level, stopping neatly next to the machine in the same place as the one the evening before. Lord Astborough stepped up to it, punched in a number on the push-button panel and the door opened. Taking hold of the door, he lifted it off its hinges and handed it to one of the two men. Polly recognised him as the heavyset man who had searched for them the night before.

"Bleeding 'ell" whispered Will, "it's another Chef!"

Polly looked at the container and gasped. The robot inside it looked exactly the same as Chef, with one quite significant difference: the top of its head was missing. Lord Astborough turned to Chef and smiled.

"It is ready and waiting for the gift you will give it."

Lord Astborough turned the man's head so that he could see the robot. Chef's eyes widened and he looked as though he was trying to speak but his body did not move.

"I know, you are wondering why you have ended up here. Simple, a pretty face turned your head. You shouldn't have been so fickle, my dear man. My temptress had tried another member of the household but he stayed loyal to his woman and you did not. So you can suffer the consequences of your betrayal. I would apologise for the pain I am about to inflict on you but then I don't care, so I won't."

Lord Astborough moved Chef's head back into place and pulled a metal bowl down over his head to just above eye level. Wires snaked out the back of it and ran over to the machine. Lord Astborough moved across to the machine, pulled down a lever and turned a dial. Within seconds Polly heard the sharp whirring of a blade. The sound changed slightly, becoming harsher and then Chef screamed.

"Oh no," Polly cried and shouted "Stop!" across the room. Lord Astborough swung round and looked up at her.

"What?" he said as he turned a switch on the wall and lights lit up along the balcony, illuminating Polly and Will. "How did you two get in here? Get them, kill them!" he shouted to his two men. "They cannot be allowed to escape, not when we are so close!"

The two men pulled out revolvers and aimed them at Polly and Will. Will started to move backward as Polly whispered a few words and sent a pulse of power toward the machine, hoping to shut it down.

"She's a witch, don't fire!" the Lord screamed but he was too late. A bullet sped from the heavyset man's gun directly toward Polly, just in time to be caught in her power spell. The bullet ricocheted away, buried itself in the machine and exploded. Polly's spell followed the bullet's path: there was a second of quiet, and then a small thump sounded as the machine cracked open, sending electricity careering outward in search of metal to spark against.

In horror, Polly saw it arc toward the table. Chef's body was lifted up from its surface. She could hear his bones cracking as the power of the electricity pulled him against the restraints before he was slammed back down again. His screams intensified as the metal heated and the stench of burning flesh filled the room. Dark lines worked across his chest as the electricity poured through him, contorting his body. She could see blood pouring from his nose and mouth as he continued to scream in agony.

Will caught hold of Polly's jacket, causing her to fall backward as bullets rained across the space where she had stood. She scrabbled after him into the corridor, desperately trying to get the last sight of Chef out of her head. She could hear the heavy footsteps of two men ringing out as they ran up the iron staircase. She blindly followed Will, still hearing Chef's screams mixing with Lord Astborough's shouted orders for the men to find them and kill them. As they ran along the corridor the now-lit lights above them began to spark and explode, causing glass fragments to rain down on top of them. They came around the bend in the corridor and saw the main door ahead of them. With no time for the key now and no need for subterfuge,

Polly sent a blast of power ahead of her. The door flew open and daylight beckoned them.

Before they could reach it though, there was an almighty BOOM, the earth shook beneath their feet and they fell to the floor. Looking behind her, Polly could see the corridor collapsing; the ceiling was falling, sending wooden beams and earth crashing to the ground. She and Will scrambled back up and rushed out onto the bank of the Serpentine as everything fell in behind them and dust spewed out, causing them to cough and gasp for air.

Polly went to run across the water but Will pulled her back and instead climbed up over the collapsed earth to the bridge. He ran across it to the other side and turned to look at her.

Polly followed fast, feeling the bridge wobbling as its support began to crumble away. Once she reached the bank, she staggered a little as she made her way up to their tree to stand beside him.

"Why did you stop us coming across the water?"

"Two reasons: one, I didn't know if the barrier was still up and what it might do to us if we tried to get across and the other, 'cause I reckon a whole lot of water is going to hit that machine in a minute and water and electricity don't mix," he said as he looked at the lake. "Oh bleeding 'ell, it's starting, come on, let's get farther up the bank and out of 'arm's way."

Polly turned and saw that the lake was rippling and churning in front of them, like water disappearing down a sink, gurgling into the sewers. Ducks and swans flew up into the air in confusion as the water disappeared beneath them. Another loud crack sounded and a geyser of water shot up, tearing the bridge apart and sending bricks and large stones slamming back down into the ever-widening hole that was emerging. The bodies of charred rats thumped into the mud next to fish left flapping as their habitat disappeared.

Then there was nothing but silence as the water poured into the hidden rooms and turned the elegant lake built for Queen Caroline into a muddy field.

The two waited but no further explosions came and nothing and no-one emerged from the hole.

"It must have burnt itself out down there, thank goodness for that, I didn't fancy having to stop people wading in there in case they was likely to get electrocuted," exclaimed Will. "There's some people coming along to investigate. I reckon it's time we took a walk away from here. I'm not sure I want to try and explain to any official personage what was going on 'ere and our part in it. I don't think they would take kindly to us blowing up the lake."

"No, I don't suppose they would. They might also get a bit awkward in regard to us not telling them earlier what Lord Astborough was up to, even though we didn't really know."

"Do you think any of them in there survived?"

"I have no idea. And we never did find out who or what the woman and child were. If Lord Astborough died in there, then his body will be recovered; if he didn't, I expect we shall hear about him again. Our more immediate problem is how on earth we are going to explain to our client that her intended was going to have his brain cut out of his living body and put into a robot as part of a plot to take down the whole British government," she said ruefully.

Will looked at her.

"I'm more interested in who is going to foot the bill to plug that 'ole, refill the lake and work out what tale they choose to explain it all away. And look on the bright side: there won't be much for her to mourn over now that he's burnt to a crisp and drowned."

"Will, that's horrible, I can still hear him screaming! He hadn't done anything wrong and my actions caused his death, I'm not going to be able to forget that."

"'ardly innocent, Polly, you 'eard the lord, that man was nothing but a player, 'appy enough to lead one woman on whilst dallying with another. As far as I'm concerned, he gives us men a bad name and deserves everything he got and if he was still alive I'd be tempted to go and finish him off myself."

Polly gave a half laugh, which caught as she remembered the way Chef's body had been flung against the restraints.

Will hugged her as he saw the tears begin to fall and smoothed her hair as she clung to him.

"Shh, Polly, it's all right, Chef didn't die because of you, he was dead the second he followed that woman."

Polly stepped back and smiled weakly up at him.

"I know, still."

He took her hand and they began to walk away as the curious began to gather.

"I wonder what our next case will bring us, 'opefully nothing quite as dramatic. I could do with a search for a lost dog after all this 'orror."

"Will, we haven't had to find a lost pet in months. I think we can aim a little higher than that."

"Except this is one we can't talk about, can we, so it might be back to the mundane jobs. We've got to eat."

"Oh, the joys of being private investigators, lost pets one month, a plot to bring down the government the next. What on earth will we have land on our laps in the future?"

"Whatever it is, Polly, you and I will solve it. The two misfits, unloved and abandoned in childhood, 'ave become a pretty impressive team, don't you think?"

"We have indeed, my friend but at this moment one-half of the impressive team is tired. Let's go home."

They left the park to the harsh sound coming from the tin whistles of the Peelers who were rushing to control the situation at the Serpentine.

THE CASE OF THE WRONG TUNE

1 TERRANCE

Polly pushed her chair back from the desk, stood up and stretched to release the tension from her back and sighed contentedly. Business had been good for her and Will over the last few months, it seemed as though a few people high up in the rich layers of society had found out about them. She had no idea how; the ways of the rich gentry was far beyond the knowledge of an orphan child brought up in the workhouse, even if she was a powerful witch. However it had happened, she was not going to complain because the rich had in the main simple problems to solve and big pockets to pay from.

She looked down at the papers she had been working on and smiled. Will's wish for a lost dog to find had been rather more accurate a predication than he could have imagined. So far, two lost Jewel's, three Major's and one Scamp had been successfully returned to their concerned owners. Though Polly was pretty certain that one of the Jewel's would be giving birth to a few surprises in a month or so.

They had managed to retrieve some actual lost jewellery, much to the relief of the accused house maid, who had been facing the eviction from her job. Overall they had managed to pull in enough money to be able to consider some new furniture for the office and their living space.

Mr Hardaker was equally pleased as he saw his sales revenue increase as more people came looking for the services of Baker & Dagger Investigators and left carrying one of his pots or pans.

She was just considering going downstairs and seeing if Will was free for a walk and a bite to eat when her buzzer sounded and she heard someone running up the stairs. She sat back down and waited to see who arrived.

The door was flung open and a thin, young man came to an abrupt halt at the sight of her.

"Oh, I'm sorry, am I in the right place; I was looking for the investigators?"

"You've found them, well one of them, I'm Pollyanne Baker and you are?"

"Oh, oh I see, I'm sorry, I didn't mean, it's just you see I've got to get someone to listen to me, no-one is listening to me, they think I'm silly, it's nothing, I should just stop worrying about it but you see there is something wrong and I can't stop being worried and something's going to happen and I don't know how to stop it." He paused as he ran out breath. Before he could start rambling again Polly went over to him, pulled him across to one of the armchairs in front of the unlit fire and gave him a gentle push to sit down. He folded down into the comfortable armchair and sat there looking awkward, one hand picking at the short nails on the other.

Polly studied him. His clothing was all black and grey. Smart, suit and waistcoat, well cared for but slightly old fashioned as though he had bought the best he could afford from a second-hand shop. His hair was dark brown, quite short but curly and was currently messy and uncontrolled. His face was pale with little round glasses perched lopsidedly on his nose, the problem stemmed from the string holding one arm of the glasses together. He looked up at her as his breathing settled, his pale hazel eyes gazing out at her in an appeal for understanding.

She smiled at him, "What is your name?"

"Oh, my name, yes of course, I'm sorry I'm most discombobulated, I don't normally do this sort of thing, I like to have a quiet life and this is most unusual."

"Your name?"

"My name, yes sorry, my name is Terrance Biggar."

"Nice to meet you Terrance, now can you start from the beginning and tell me what you are concerned about?"

"Yes, um well, the beginning, hmm, I suppose it started a few weeks ago. At first I didn't notice, I mean why would you? You see that sort of person all the time, all over the city, you hardly notice them anymore; just maybe throw a few coins if you feel like it but really they are insignificant."

"Who are?" asked Polly beginning to feel a bit exasperated with the young man.

"What?" said Terrance.

"Who are insignificant?"

"Oh, didn't I say what he was?

"No."

"I am sorry; I really am not certain what is wrong I just strongly feel that something is, you see he's playing the wrong tune. Yes that's it, it's almost right but there's a few notes that don't fit and I feel odd when he plays them as though they are hurting me almost. Does that sound strange?"

"My dear Terrance, so far everything you have said sounds strange. Please tell me this, who is playing the wrong tune?"

"I'm not doing this very well am I? Normally I work with numbers, they're simple see, they all follow in line and if one gets lost somewhere I can find it, I'm very good at finding lost numbers but words, they tumble out of me and get mixed up all the time."

Polly just smiled at him; hopefully if he rambled enough she might pick up what he was concerned about.

"Right, the wrong tune, who's playing it, I can answer that one. It's an organ grinder and he has a monkey, horrible little menace, it chatters away and screeches at people as they pass by. I really don't know how he puts up with it, ugly scrap of an animal, very dirty."

"Or maybe not", she thought and tried to steer him back to the main point.

"So an organ grinder and monkey have set up a pitch near where you work?"

"Yes, yes that's it, you've got it and he's playing the wrong tune."

"I've got that much yes. Now where do you work?"

"In the city, the Whithersnick Bank, it's a small establishment, nowhere near as big as the Rothschild's bank next door but I like working there."

"How long have you been there?"

"Years, they took me on as an office boy and I've worked my way up to Accounting Clerk."

"Well done, sounds admirable. Now when did the Organ Grinder first appear?"

"I didn't really notice him at first, it was only when I realised the tune had changed. So I guess he had been there a few days before but then this time as I walked past him the tune sounded horrible so I turned to look at him and the monkey screeched and made me jump. I hurried away from him and didn't think anything of it, until the same thing happened the next morning. Then I started to wonder what was happening and I took to watching him out of my window. If I sat at the very edge of my desk I could just see him as he walked back and forth."

"When was this, Terrance?" Polly asked beginning to wonder if she would ever catch hold of the facts.

Terrance must have picked up on her annoyance, because his shoulders slumped a little and he went to stand up.

"You don't believe me either, I'm sorry I've wasted your time, I will go."

"Terrance, please sit down. It is not a case of whether I believe you or not, it is more that I have no idea what you are trying to explain to me. Now as far as I can glean from your conversation you work in a bank and sometime in the last few weeks an Organ Grinder has set up a stall near your office. All was fine until one day he did something that upset you and now you believe that he is up to no good. Am I on the right track?"

"Yes, that's it's exactly but it's not that I believe he's up to no good, I'm sure of it. You see I've watched him, he's making notes, he's watching the bank, I think he means to break into it and steal something from our vaults."

"Why haven't any of your work colleagues realised this, haven't they seen him making notes? Surely you have someone that is concerned with security in your bank that would take your concerns seriously?"

"That's just it, they won't, they keep saying I'm imagining things, that he's not doing any harm and the monkey is charming and it's nice to have a bit of music to entertain them during the day. It's like I'm the only one that can hear the wrong tune and see the truth of the matter."

"What made you come here today?"

Terrance ran his fingers through his hair.

"I heard something last night. I was in the office late, because I had work I could do and also because I wanted to wait until the Organ Grinder had gone. So I was on my own with just one small light on, enough to let me see my work but not enough to light the area outside my little booth. I was tired and must have dozed off for a bit, because I woke up to find my light had gone out and it was pitch dark outside. I reached across my desk to pick up a spare candle I keep for such occasions and was about to light it when I heard voices."

He stopped and looked at Polly.

"I really didn't mean to eavesdrop on a private conversation but once I realised who it was I couldn't open my mouth to tell them I was there."

"Who was it?"

"Mr Whithersnick Jnr and Mr Belton, the head of security."

"I can see why you stayed quiet. What did you hear?"

"It didn't make sense; Mr Whithersnick asked if everything was ready for the delivery. Mr Belton assured him that it was and further precautions had been put into place."

"What sort of precautions?"

"I don't know, we don't keep much at the bank, a supply of gold for any day to day transactions and there is the deposit box room but that is kept locked and only Mr Whithersnick Snr has a key for that and he is always attended by Mr Belton. That is where things are kept for customers who do not wish to keep things of value in their homes."

"And so you think something is being delivered to be stored in that room and whatever it is, it is what the Organ Grinder is interested in."

"Yes, exactly, no one would bother breaking into our bank for money, there isn't enough there to make it worth their while, we have tight security and anyone found trying to break in, doesn't get reported to the Peelers, they are dealt with by Mr Belton and his guards. I don't think they are very nice to them."

Polly stood up and went to the window and looked out thinking for a moment. Thankfully Terrance stayed quiet as she pondered the situation.

Turning back to him she smiled.

"I take it you are currently on your lunch break?"

"Yes, I need to get back soon, I don't think it would look good if I was missed."

"Of course, well Terrance, go back to work and rest assured that I shall investigate this Organ Grinder for you and with any luck I will discover that he is nothing more than a bad tune smith."

Terrance rose and moved over the door.

"Thank you, I don't know how I can pay you for anything you do, I don't earn very much money."

"Do not worry, I will take this case as being one that is handed to me by a concerned citizen. No fee required."

With a final nod of thanks, Terrance left ran back down the stairs and Polly watched through the window as he ran down the street back towards the city.

"What did he want?" said Will coming into the office. "Must be pretty important he was 'ere for ages."

"I have no idea, Will, most of the time he was just gabbling, however, I think Gadget and I should take a wander down to the banking area."

"Can't you take me?"

"There's a problem with an Organ Grinder and his monkey near the Whithersnick Bank. Now if something nefarious is going on, I wouldn't like to draw attention to myself. And a wolf, however human he may be, walking near a monkey is bound to cause a scene."

"True, blimey the fuss those monkeys made when we went to the zoo."

"Indeed and Gadget has wanted to play a bigger part in our investigations, this could be the perfect chance. I don't envisage much danger can occur to us wandering through the streets of the city in broad daylight and if I think I will need you, I can send Gadget back to get you."

"Whatever you do, don't take any chances; I don't want Gadget getting to me too late."

"I won't, now whilst we are out investigating the Organ Grinder, there is something you could be doing."

"What?"

"Get yourself along to Companies House and see what you can find out about the Whithersnick Bank. Who are the controlling parties, it sounds a family affair from Terrance's description, so see if you can find out who sits on the board. See who backed them, if something is going on, then we need to know who they are affiliated with."

"You reckon something is up then?"

"I don't know but better we find the information out now then have to go hunting it later. If Terrance is right and he's hearing something that no-one else is, then it could be within our realm of expertise."

"Let's have some lunch first and then we can go looking for information this afternoon. It will also give your young client a chance to get back to the office so if anything does happen he won't be caught up in it."

The two of them walked downstairs and Will went to tell Gadget about the job they felt she could do whilst Polly apologised to Mr Hardaker for leaving him short-handed for the afternoon.

"Don't you be worrying Miss Polly, I'll be 'appy to get young Gadget out of my 'air, she's been driving me insane with changes to me shop all day."

"She is one for sorting things out Mr Hardaker," Polly said as Gadget came running in and then sighed with despair as she saw how the girl was dressed, "couldn't you find something nicer to wear?"

Gadget stood there in worn out brown boots beneath rolled up brown trousers, which were belted in at her waist because they were far too big for her. A white collarless shirt was tucked into the trousers and a brown waistcoat was open and unbuttoned showing a few dirty marks on the shirt front. A blue scarf knotted at her throat and a flat cap covering her short hair completed the look. A leather satchel was flung across her body and odd bulges showed pushing out against the side.

"What's wrong with this, perfect disguise," she said on seeing Polly's horrified expression "I look like your younger brother and anyway people are far less discreet around young boys than they should be. It's more comfortable than anything else anyway and if I can get away with people thinking I'm a boy then who cares. If'n you need me to run back for Will I ain't going to manage it in any hoity toity dress now am I?" She said as a final reason.

"Enough. One day Gadget you will want to put on a dress."

"Not bleeding likely," she retorted.

"Very well, enough arguing, I'm hungry and it's time for lunch. Would you like some soup and bread Mr Hardaker, I believe there is still some in the larder."

"Can't we go now?" asked Gadget.

"It wouldn't be worth it, Terrance says the Organ Grinder is there all day, if we go now we will have to stand and watch him for hours. If we have food first we can go along, maybe sit in a tea shop for a little so as to observe him, though they may not let you in looking like that."

"Alright then, I can wait but I'm not changing."

An hour later, Gadget was running out the front door, calling that she would hail a cab and would Polly please hurry.

Polly and Will followed her out and caught up with her as she was hailing down a cab. Polly climbed up into it after telling the cabbie where they wanted to go. Gadget was already in and bouncing on the seats in excitement.

Will looked up at Polly as he closed the cab door.

"Have fun; suddenly Companies House seems quite restful."

Polly smiled at him and turned to tell Gadget to sit properly as the horses began to move them forward.

2 THE ORGAN GRINDER

Polly stood across the road and a little way back from where the Organ Grinder, accompanied by his monkey, had set up his dilapidated music organ. It was balanced precariously on a three-legged wooden stand, one leg of which was broken and wound round with wire to hold it together. She was close enough to see them quite clearly and hoped she was just far enough away that her study of the pair would not be noticed.

The monkey was scrawny and small, screeching and chattering at passers-by just as Terrance had described. It had a trick of holding out one hand in supplication, whilst the other held tight to a tin can with a hole in the top for coins. He proffered the can in front of anyone who stopped, as though it was he that needed the money and not his owner. He was wearing a faded red waistcoat with what would once have been bright gold piping running around its edges, now broken threads hung like faded golden cobwebs. On his head was a small round red hat with a tassel hanging from its centre, again faded and damaged like the piping.

His owner did not look much better. A small man, his back a little bent implying that he had spent years leaning over to turn the handle so to produce the cracked sound that emanated from his music box. His trousers and shirt would have once been black but were now a muddy grey and the same wear and tear showed on his red waistcoat, matching his monkey. In an addition he had around his throat a bright red and gold scarf that trailed down over the front of the waistcoat. His thinning hair was long and tied back with a leather thong, though strands of it escaped to fall about his face and his goatee beard was grey and thinning. To the casual observer his whole appearance portrayed a man who had spent years plying his trade as a music man but whilst she watched Polly was aware that he was alert and aware of everything around him. Whatever the faded façade showed to the passing public behind it was a brain as sharp as a pin.

Gadget standing next to her was fidgeting with impatience.

"Can't I just walk past, I want to hear the music better."

"Why, it sounds awful here, do we need to get closer, he might realise that we are watching him and become wary."

"I didn't mean both of us to go, just me. I have something that might explain why his music upset Terrance so much."

"Really, what?"

Gadget dug into her bag and pulled out a small box that had two metal rods pushed into the top with wire connecting them at the tips. The box had a marked half circle with a wire indicator in the middle.

"What on earth have you got there?" asked Polly.

"It's something I made ages ago and when Will told me we were investigating someone playing the wrong tune or something like that I thought I would bring it with me. You see music makes the wire shake and the vibrations goes down the metal rods and they move the indicator. If the note is a good one, the needle goes to the right and if it is flat or sharp it goes to the left."

"And what will that tell us and how are you going to use it without alerting the suspicions of the organ grinder?"

"Easy", said Gadget and pulled out a sandwich wrapped in grease proof paper, "I'm going to go over and sit near him as though enjoying the music whilst I eat my food, I will put my bag on the ground with my gadget behind it and watch the needle move. Then when I've finished my sandwich I can put a penny into the can and come back and tell you what I think."

Without waiting to hear whether Polly approved of her plan, Gadget moved away and sauntered over to the Organ Grinder. She went up to him and smiled, said something to the man, to which he nodded and smiled. Then she shook the hand of the monkey and sat down far enough away from them to not impede their business but close enough to carry out her plan.

Polly did have to admit to herself that it was as smooth a play as anything she could have done so she wandered away a bit further, found a bench to sit down on and waited for Gadget to finish her sandwich. Taking out a small book from her pocket she pretended to read whilst occasionally looking up to check on Gadget.

She was just considering going over and pulling Gadget away by her ear when she saw her get up, shake the hand of the monkey again, put a penny in the can and walk back towards her. Without stopping or looking at Polly, she said as she passed her.

"He will be watching me walk away, I'll wait for you round the next corner."

She carried on walking to the end of the road, turned back, waved to the

Organ Grinder, who waved back in return, then disappeared. Polly waited a few moments, checked to see that the man and monkey weren't looking her way and then followed.

Gadget was beaming with excitement when Polly caught up with her, she was leaning against a lamppost a few yards back from the turn in the street.

"Well?" said Polly.

"He's not a real Organ Grinder."

"I do hope you don't tell me it's not a real monkey either."

"Of course it's a real monkey and it's a well-trained one at that, because both of them are pretending. There's only one thing wrong with the music box, one of the hammers is not hitting the right spot and I could fix it in five minutes if they would let me but he wasn't picking up that it was wrong, so they're not real. No true music man would let his box be used if it was damaged like that."

"So that's all that's wrong with it, a fault in the music box?"

"Yes, though why a note being wrong would upset Terrance so much I have no idea."

"Well it could be actually be something very simple. His world revolves around numbers and them being in the right place, in the right order. So if we think of a tune being a set of notes in the right order then if one note is wrong it's going to upset him, add in the monkey frightening him…."

"Of course, I get it, add it together and it would upset him enough that he begins to notice other things that are wrong?"

"Yes, absolutely, I expect that the Organ Grinder is being very careful to hide what he is doing but if someone is already thinking that something is wrong and is keeping a look out of their window, they might well notice other things."

"What are we going to do now?"

"We aren't going to do anything, you are going to get back to the office to wait for Will and I am going to follow the Organ Grinder when he packs up for the day. I doubt he is the main player in this scheme, whatever it is, so he will report to someone higher up the chain and that's who I want to find out about."

Gadget went to complain but Polly put up a hand to stop her.

"You've already done brilliantly but now the Organ Grinder will recognise you, I can't let him see you with me. You've done enough for today, go home and see if you can manage to not annoy Mr Hardaker any more today."

Gadget looked at her and shrugged.

"I only ever suggest things that would help him. He's so old fashioned. Are you sure you'll be alright? I don't want to leave you alone out here, you might need some protection."

Polly laughed, "I won't need protecting, I have plenty of tricks up my sleeve, don't you worry. Now get on back."

Polly hailed a passing hansom cab, pushed Gadget up into the seat next to the driver and paid the fare to get her back to the office.

"I'll see you later," she said and waved the cabby to get going. Once he had turned out of sight, she went back to the corner of the road and looked round carefully. The Organ Grinder and his monkey were still there plying their trade. Polly went into a tea shop along the street, ordered a pot of tea and cake and settled down at a table in the window to watch him.

After an hour she saw what looked like bank staff begin to leave the Whithersnick bank for the day and quite a few put some pennies into the can. She caught sight of Terrance and smiled as she saw him make a wide berth of the man and even go as far as to make the sign of the cross as though to ward off evil. A movement that the Organ Grinder didn't see or if he did made no sign of reply.

The crowds quickly dispersed though as the light began to fade and Polly could hear the lamplighters beginning to walk along and light up the gas lamps. The quick burst of gas followed by the soft whump sound as the flame caught hold. She watched as the Organ Grinder packed up the music box, using straps on it to pull it on his back. He folded down the legs and used a cord along them to sling them on to his right shoulder and the monkey scrambled up and sat on the other. He began to walk straight towards where Polly was sitting in the shop.

Leaning forward so that he wouldn't notice her through the thick glass, she watched him through the corner of her eye as he passed her by. Oblivious now it seemed to everyone around him, he was nothing more than a man at the end of his working day intent on getting home to food and warmth as soon as possible. Polly though, remembering how alert he had been earlier was not so easily fooled. As he went past her she got up and left the tea shop. Looking down the road she caught sight of the monkey on his shoulder and began to follow. In order to escape his detection she whispered a charm that would disguise her a little. It wouldn't hide her from everyone, she had tried that once and found that everyone kept bumping into her and exclaiming because they couldn't work out what had happened. It seemed that bumping into thin air disturbed people, so she had instead perfected a charm that let people see a person but not register any details of who it was, either male, female, tall, short, fat or thin, just a blob in front of them to be avoided.

Once the charm was fully established she worked her way closer to the Organ Grinder and it wasn't long before she realised where they were heading. To Soho, not a part of town she really wanted to visit, as it was renowned as the area for criminals, prostitutes and those wanting to hide from the world. Drugs were rife, opium dens spewed sickly bitter-sweet smoke out of vents and drains, promising release to the lost and the hopeless and warning the healthy to take a wide berth round them. Though in the dark and tight alleyways of Soho a wide berth was very rarely available. The dregs of the city survived in overcrowded hovels, houses where the cellars were always damp and the brickwork crumbled, as cracked windows let the cold wind blow through. People very rarely escaped from Soho; once entered it was a strong person who could climb out of the filth.

But Polly needed to find out the next link of the chain so as she reached the outer limits of Soho, she strengthened the charm around her and followed the Organ Grinder into the dark small streets.

He seemed unaffected by the dingy and filthy streets around him and continued confidently turning left and right in a dizzying route which almost had Polly losing her bearings. However while she now lived and worked in a nicer part of town, her childhood had showed her this sort of world and the sights and sounds did not make her lose her sense of direction. As she went further and further in she still felt confident of her ability to escape back to the safer areas again. She could hear the sound of music and laughter wafting towards them and the Organ Grinder went towards it. He turned a corner with Polly close behind him and there in front of them was a large three storey inn from where light shone out from windows. Above the entrance a sign hung down of a corpse dancing in a noose, the name on the sign was "The Hangman's Dance". Polly looked at it in disgust, it seemed to thumb a nose at the possibility of death and sneer at the authorities that enforced the law. She almost missed seeing the Organ Grinder disappear along the right-hand side of the building and go down a flight of steps, she followed after him and looked down as he disappeared through a door at the bottom of the steps.

Polly hesitated but as no-one seemed to have noticed her she followed down the steps, her footsteps light and making no sound as she descended. Half way down she stopped, a small window was ajar and she watched as the Organ Grinder came into view, took off his music box and placed it on the ground and let the monkey jump down from his shoulder. He grimaced a little and rubbed the small of his back, then moved out of her sight but came back to sit down in a chair holding a glass of wine. The monkey climbed up into his lap and pulled at the glass, the Organ Grinder smiled and let the monkey have a drink before pulling it away from him, waiting a moment and then taking a large mouthful himself.

"Thank you kindly, Mr Innocent," he said, "after the day I've had, a vintage of this quality is most welcome."

"Yet you let the monkey try it first," a warm voice replied, though from Polly's vantage point she could not see the speaker. She just had the feeling that the man was smiling and inwardly laughing at the Organ Grinder.

"Force of 'abit, I'm afraid," the Organ Grinder replied, "the life of a monkey is short, so if anything should 'appen to him, no real 'arm done but I would 'ate to find myself suffering from a bad wine, if you take my meaning my good Sir."

"You are working for me, why would I want to harm you?"

"Always found it good, in my business to be careful, that's all Sir, no insult intended".

"None taken" the voice replied dryly.

There was something about the voice that made Polly wish she could see the speaker, a hint of class and intelligence, a sense that the speaker had looked at the world and decided to mock it.

"So what did you find out today, what is there to report?" the voice asked.

"Sir, I reckon the gold is being brought in tomorrow. I over'eard a few of the workers saying that there 'ad been lots of toing and froing today and 'ow Mr Whithersnick Jnr was looking most perturbed."

"Well, that is a sign of something happening, Mr Whithersnick Jnr being perturbed. Seriously why tomorrow?"

"Because Mr Innocent, Sir, one of the young men in talking to his friend whilst my monkey climbed all over him, said that there was going to be an important delivery made on Friday and it's Friday tomorrow."

"Tomorrow. You didn't think to warn me about the delivery being on Friday a bit earlier?"

The Organ Grinder winced.

"I'm sorry Sir, I didn't know until today, I mean nobody was saying anything in front of me for ages, they 'ad to get used to me being there and start to ignore me."

"Hmm" was all the sound that came back to him.

"So that's what this is all about," thought Polly, a bank robbery but strange that the Organ Grinder was saying that gold was being delivered when Terrance had told her that the bank never held much gold. Maybe something else was being delivered but if that was the case why wasn't the Organ Grinder telling Mr Innocent, whoever he was, the truth. "To follow the argument on," she continued to herself, "if the Organ Grinder isn't telling this man the truth, is he really working for him and if he isn't working for him, who is he working for?"

She moved closer to the window to see if she could see anything more and watched as the Organ Grinder took off his scarf and leant down to place it on his music box. She gasped as she saw on the back of his neck a brand. Almost nothing more than a semi-circular scar with an odd wavy line through it but she had seen the same marking once before, as a doodle in some accounting books, on her and Will's first foray under the Serpentine.

"So he didn't die", she thought to herself. Lord Astborough had survived and now however much Mr Innocent believed the Organ Grinder was sourcing information for him, something else was going on underneath it all. "And whatever that is, it won't be good, for Mr Innocent or anyone else." She was just considering whether she had seen and heard enough and whether she ought to go back and discuss the whole situation with Will when she became aware of the light dimming behind her. She looked back up the stairs and saw at the top of the stairs one of biggest men she had ever seen.

"Never mind", she thought, "he can't see me, I will just wait, I'm sure he will move on in a minute."

But he didn't, the man came down the stairs, Polly went to move away from him but he moved too quickly and suddenly she found her arm held by a hand that seemed bigger than her head.

"Alright whoever you are, don't you be worried about anything but Mr Innocent doesn't like eavesdroppers much, especially ones that use magic to hide themselves and so I reckon he will want to know what you were doing listening in on his private conversation."

Polly tried to free her arm but it was held firmly, there was no escape from this man's grasp. He kept hold and pulled her down the rest of the steps to the door at the bottom.

3 MR INNOCENT AND COLOSSUS

"Who are you and what are you doing here?" the man asked.

Polly was too amazed that the man had seen her and realised she was using magic to say anything.

The man took her through the door, along a short corridor and then stopped outside a shut door.

"We'll just let Mr Innocent say goodbye to his first visitor, no need to let him know you were listening in on the conversation."

The man let go of her arm and turned to look down at her, he squinted a little as though trying to focus on her.

"Now don't you go worrying yourself none, I'm not about to hurt you any, so would you be so good as to drop your charm, I would like to see who I'm about to introduce myself to."

Polly looked up at him and almost had to send her neck as far back as she could to see his face. He was massive, she reckoned at least four or five inches taller than Will but more than that, his shoulders almost filled the corridor and his body was a thick and solid looking as a tree trunk. That he was black added to her immediate image of standing in front of an oak tree. He smiled and bright white teeth flashed as his eyes crinkled and showed laugh lines. Polly relaxed, massive he might be but she could pick up no vibrations of harm from him. He tentatively put out a hand to shake hers and Polly dropped the charm to place her hand in his.

The man looked down at her and a wide smile came onto his face.

"Well, that's a nice surprise, hello Miss, didn't expect to see someone as pretty as you in this hell hole. My name is Col, Miss, short for Colossus, I'm afraid that's the only name I know, can't remember what my mother called me, can't remember my mother so I don't suppose it really matters much what I'm called."

"I'm Pollyanne Baker, Col, nice to meet you." She went to shake his hand and almost laughed as looked down and saw that his hand engulfed hers but he matched his strength to hers and gravely shook her hand in welcome. Small scars crisscrossed over his knuckles and as she looked back up to his face, she saw further scars slashing across his cheekbones. She was about to say something when the door flew open and she jumped back in surprise.

"If you could stop lollygagging with our visitor Col, I would like to find out what is going on."

Polly turned to look at the man standing in the doorway but with the light from inside the room she couldn't work out what he looked like. She was though fully aware of his anger, it was rolling off him and she tried to back away but the solid form of Col behind pushed her into the room. Before she could bump into the man he turned, stalked back to a large desk at the back of the room and leant against it looking at her.

Polly stumbled a little and then pulled herself upright. "Demmed if I'm going to let him scare me," she thought to herself.

The man said nothing, just studied her as she stood in front of him, so Polly did the same thing and watched as he got more annoyed with her not saying anything. "He's actually quite attractive," she thought "though he would look better if he smiled."

In any normal company, she thought, he would be considered tall but compared to Colossus behind her he seemed short and he was probably an inch or so shorter than Will. Which still put him much taller than herself. His hair was straight and black, cut to just above his shoulders. In the dim light of the room she couldn't see what colour eyes he had. He was frowning at her but small lines showed at the corners of his eyes and his mouth was almost betraying his anger and trying to curl into a smile of welcome as he took in her appearance. His clothing was plain and well made, his velvet waistcoat was new and well cut not ostentatious, no extra braiding or lace filigree added to it but still she could tell expensive. What was he doing in an establishment like this one? He obviously finished his summing up of her before she did of him, because he broke the silence first.

"Well, what were you doing listening in up there?"

Polly hesitated considering whether to spin a line to him but then thought the truth would probably serve her better.

"I was following the Organ Grinder, I wanted to know what he was doing."

"And do you now know?"

"Maybe but it isn't what you think he's doing?"

The man looked over at Colossus and raised an eyebrow in question but Colossus just shrugged.

"I don't know how much she heard Innocent, I just came round the corner and was aware of the magic tint in the air, so I came down and found her."

The man looked back at Polly and suddenly his anger disappeared. He smiled and Polly thought "I'm right; he is attractive when he smiles."

He put a hand out to shake hers and said.

"You seem to have me at a disadvantage then, if you know something I don't, I would like to know it. Let me introduce myself, I'm known as Mr Innocent. Friends call me Innocent or Inno, I don't really mind. And you are?"

Polly took his hand and shook it.

"I'm Pollyanne Baker, my friends call me Polly and I'm part of Baker and Dagger Investigators, though I wouldn't presume for us to be friends quite yet."

"Feisty isn't she Col. You're an investigator? Rather small, young and female for that task aren't you?"

"You forget the magic part that your friend detected; it does tend to level the playing field sometimes."

"I guess it would, I don't have that skill, neither actually does my friend, Col. There is magic in him I'm sure, not to use but he can sense it, which helps a lot in my line of work," he turned and gestured to some chairs laid out near a lit fire, "would you care to sit down and we can continue this conversation in comfort."

Polly went over and sat down and Innocent sat down opposite her. Col remained near the doorway, so however much she was being welcomed and dealt with in a kindly manner, Polly was aware that escape from the room would be a little problematic. Possible of course, because however big Colossus was a power surge would move him but there were things she wanted to find out, so she was happy enough to continue with the game.

"Now what is it that you think you know that I don't?" asked Innocent.

"You think the Organ Grinder is working for you, I don't," Polly replied.

"Of course he's working for me, I'm paying him."

"And he brings you such good information, there is gold being delivered, oh and he just found out it's tomorrow. How much planning time has he given you, almost none, you will be going into that bank blind Mr Innocent, with no idea of exactly what you are looking for. You are being swindled and played because there is some else he is answering to."

"Who and why are you so sure of it?"

"The who is someone that I hoped had died, why is because of two things, one I have it on good authority that there is very little gold in the Whithersnick bank and two I saw a brand on his neck."

"That is very little to go on, a bank always has some gold and maybe some more is being deposited."

"I agree that the bank is getting a delivery but if it's the person who I think is involved, the delivery will not be anything of monetary value, it will be something far more dangerous and you are being used as a scapegoat or sacrificial lamb."

Innocent looked at her for a long moment and then laughed out loud, sprang up from the chair went over to his desk poured a glass of wine and downed it in one go. Then he poured out a further glass for himself and another that he brought over and gave to Polly. He sat back down and placed the wine glass on a side table next to his chair.

"Thank you Polly, I don't think I have ever been described in such a way. I have never considered myself a domestic farm animal before now, I would rather think of myself as a predator. And I must point out that the person, if there is such a one that is putting me into that role must be extremely devious because I sought out the Organ Grinder, I sent him to the Whithersnick Bank and he reports to me. So how could someone else have manufactured all that?"

Polly considered him for a moment whilst she let her mind worry the point. Then she smiled.

"Did you pick up the rumour about the delivery to the bank through contacts, through over hearing whispers in the inn and then did you also learn of a person that could be paid to watch, to take notes in the same way, through not one person but whispers and sidelong comments from many? What's the easiest way to hide your true purpose but by making the other person think they are making all the moves?"

"She's good, Innocent and that's a valid point," said Colossus.

"Thank you, yes, no need to take her side, let me think about this for a bit."

He got up and paced back and forth across the room for a while before stopping and coming back to his chair. He sat down, picked up his glass of wine, took a sip of it and looked back at her.

"One more question, who then do you believe is behind this?"

Polly paused and took a sip of her wine, then another in appreciation of its quality, before placing it down on the side table next to her chair and looking back at him.

"I believe it to be Lord Astborough."

Innocent laughed again.

"Really, Lord Astborough, are you sure, he tried to come back a few months ago and then disappeared, no-one's heard or seen him since. It can't be him; he was always a fool even before the debacle of his father's financial demise."

"Nevertheless, I believe it is him and if it is I warn you to tread very carefully, whatever you think is in that bank isn't and there is something else that he desires and he will happily kill in order to get what he wants."

"You raise some interesting points and I must think on what you have said. But the questions I must ask myself is how do you know that? And can I trust you? My colleague catches you listening at the window, you could be trying to put me off the scent in order to achieve your own goals."

Polly went to say something but Innocent put up his hand to stop her and made a small noise of annoyance. Polly stared at him in amazement, how dare he tell her to be quiet in such a fashion. This was proving to be a most annoying encounter and the sooner she could get out the better. She wanted nothing to do with this insolent man however much she liked the way the light from the fire played across the strong lines in his face. Now where did that come from, she thought to herself.

Innocent got up from his chair and started pacing again, swapping glances with Colossus and then stopping to look at Polly and then pacing for a bit more before finally leaning back against the table again.

"This is how I figure it," he said "either you are exactly what you say you are and someone has come to you with concerns about the Organ Grinder, so you watched him at the bank today, followed him here and overheard or saw something that convinced you that he is working against me. Or you are working for the bank and know about the delivery and are trying to convince me that there is nothing there, so that I won't go ahead with my plan to relieve the bank of its wealth."

"Why do you think I would be working for the bank?"

"Because my dear you have the best disguise possible."

"What?"

"Send a pretty girl to someone like me and surely I'll believe any tale she tells me."

"Except you do not believe the truth that I am trying to tell you. If Lord Astborough is involved you are in serious danger. He is prepared to kill for what he wants and I have seen that for myself."

Innocent smiled "Note that she's not denying that she's pretty though, is she Col?"

"Oh for goodness sake, if you are not going to listen to me then I'm leaving." Polly stood up from the chair and went up to Colossus. "If you don't mind, I need to get home, it's been a long day and I'm tired."

Colossus looked over her shoulder to Innocent.

"It's fine, let her go but Polly remember this, if you interfere with my plans or inform anyone of what you heard tonight I will be very annoyed."

"I will certainly be discussing your ridiculous attitude with my business partner and we will attempt to discover where Lord Astborough is and what his plans are. If we can stop him achieving his purpose that will be enough for us, if that also foils you in your attempt to steal from the bank, so be it."

Innocent walked over to Polly and looked at her, his gaze resting on her and he raised a hand to touch her cheek.

"Please do not try to cross me, it would be a shame to hurt someone as pretty as you but do not think I am a gentleman, I gave up any right to that title years ago, it is a hard world we live in and I aim to take what I want when I want it. Take care Pollyanne Baker, take care."

He bent down and gently kissed her, before abruptly turning away. Polly stared at his back half tempted to turn him into a jackass for taking such liberties, though her body was still tingling from his touch.

"Escort her out Col and ensure she leaves Soho safe and sound."

"Yes Innocent. Come along Miss Baker."

He took hold of Polly's arm and steered her out of the room and up the stairs.

"You can let go of my arm Colossus, there is no need to lead me out of Soho, I got in here safely enough and I can get myself out, I'm not a weak damsel in distress, I have powers of my own thank you."

"Innocent told me to get you out of Soho and I don't like to disappoint him Miss Baker, so we will just take a stroll together like friends would and you can tell me more about this Lord Astborough and what you think might happen. See sometimes Innocent doesn't want to hear things that I think are important, so sometimes it works better that I listen, see?"

They began to walk away from the noise of the pub and back into the dark alleyways.

"Who is he Colossus and why that name?"

"Innocent, well it's a bit of joke really Miss, he gave up his old name and no I'm not going to tell you what that is. He might one day, seeing how he seemed to take a bit of shine to you but that is his story to tell not mine. Anyway it was something someone said one day, how he was always innocent, no one ever accused him of anything and even if they did, nothing could ever be proved, so he took that as his name. Mr Innocent, because he isn't see?"

"Seems a little perverse but I suppose it's as good a name as any, how about yours?"

"Well mine is more truthful like, I guess if I went the same way as Mr Innocent I'd be called Tiny but Colossus works better, I get to instill a bit of fear before I have to do anything, sometimes solves things before I have to lay a finger on someone."

"You're his enforcer then?"

Polly was aware that as they were walking along people were melting away from Colossus; she had never walked so easily through the crowded Soho streets.

"Sometimes but Mr Innocent doesn't like to work that way, he says violence is the last thing that should happen, he likes to think things out, sort all the problems out first so that violence won't be necessary. He also reckons kindness works better, will get you more loyalty in the long run."

"Is that why you are with him?"

"Kindness? I suppose it could be or might have been in the beginning but now, no now he's like my brother, he needs me as much as I need him. Enough of me and Innocent, what did you see that made you so sure Lord Astborough is involved."

Colossus steered her away from a group of men that were quarrelling over a game of dice. As they went past Polly heard the sound of a knife clearing leather and knew that someone wouldn't get home tonight. For all her belief in her own ability it was nice to have the solid shape of Colossus next to her.

"Because the young man that came to me told me that the bank never held much gold but he had overheard the Security Chief and the younger Mr Whithersnick discuss a delivery that required precautions. Then when I followed the Organ Grinder here I saw on the back of his neck a brand, it was an image that I associate with Lord Astborough."

"It still might be something of value being delivered; the story goes that the late unlamented Lord Astborough lost all the family wealth but that could be a lie, maybe the incumbent Lord Astborough wants to protect what is left."

Polly shook her head "Lord Astborough isn't after money or gold, he wants to destroy those who he sees as being responsible for his current position. Whatever is being delivered is something else entirely, a weapon of some sort, a source of power, I don't know what but your Mr Innocent is being led down a very dangerous path Colossus, you must get him to leave that bank alone."

"I'm afraid that won't happen, he can see the wealth already in his hands Miss Polly, nothing's going to stop him trying to get it."

She stopped walking as she realised they had reached the wide-open streets that bordered Soho. She looked up at Colossus.

"Then keep your eyes open for magic or treachery Colossus because there will be some involved and you could both get burnt."

"I'll do my best Miss Polly, it's what I'm there for. I trust that if we meet again it will be under nicer circumstances."

He held his hand out and Polly shook it as she considered his face. There was power there, she thought and danger but also a strong feeling of protection surrounded the tall man.

"I hope we meet again Colossus, good luck" she said and turned away from him to walk over to where a line of hansom cabs were standing waiting for a fair. She climbed up into the first one and was soon on her way back towards the office.

\#\#\#

Will was waiting for her half asleep in one of the chairs, his long legs stretched out in front of him and a stripped chicken bone left on a plate on the desk was evidence of a cold supper. He opened one eye and regarded her.

"So the monkey didn't eat you then?"

"No, I survived the monkey, in fact I don't think the monkey ever noticed me."

"Must 'ave been a pretty blind monkey then. But something 'appended, you can't tell me you've been following the Organ Grinder all evening. Anyway you've got that air about you."

"What air?"

"The one that tells me you 'ave an inkling as to what's going on."

"I'm not completely sure but I have a feeling I know who we're up against."

"Will you let me hazard a guess?"

"Of course I will but let me sit down and have a bite to eat, I'm starving."

"I'll make you up a plate. Sit down and I'll get it for you."

Will disappeared out of the door and she heard him run up the stairs to their small kitchen. He had returned by the time she had taken off her jacket, loosened the lacing of her corset and sunk down with a sigh of contentment into the other arm chair.

Will handed her the plate with a flourish along with a napkin. Polly took the plate gratefully, picked up a leg of chicken and looked across at Will as he sat down.

"Thank you for this. So your guess?"

"Someone we 'oped had died," he said looking expectantly at her, "our friend Lord Astborough."

"How did you come by that revelation?"

"Amazing what you can find out when you talk nice enough to a young lady. Seems the Board of the Whithersnick Bank has had a few changes over the last couple of years. Turns out when it started the current Lord Astborough's father was on it, then he was got rid of and all mention of the Astborough name in connection with the bank was blacked out. It was only that she 'ad found one place where they 'adn't that she knew about it. I'm guessing from your lack of surprise you reckon it's 'im as well, 'ow did you find out?"

"A brand on the neck of the Organ Grinder, to most people it wouldn't mean a thing but it looked like a mark in the book we looked at in that room under the Serpentine. Plus what he was saying to the next person in the chain, didn't ring true so I was pretty certain that he was playing a double game and that Lord Astborough is setting someone else up to take the fall for anything that happens at the Whithersnick Bank."

"'ow did you 'ear him talking to the next person in the chain?"

"Never leave a window open if you don't want someone to listen in Will. Though I did get caught out."

"That was careless of you."

"Not completely, I had used my cover charm, turns out that the crime lord in Soho has a bodyguard that can sense magic being used, so I got to meet Mr Innocent and Colossus. I did tell them what I thought but Mr Innocent was not amenable to my reasoning."

"He's real then, Mr Innocent? I've 'eard a few whisperings about 'im but thought it was just talk, along with talk about a killer that is his second in command."

"No, he's real and a bit of an enigma. I am tempted to try and save him from his folly. He seemed rather too good a man, for all his position and obviously nefarious way of life to be played by someone as despicable as Lord Astborough."

"As long as we mess up the plans of Lord Astborough, I don't mind who else we 'elp. But what are we going to do? We don't know when the delivery that Terrance overheard being discussed is going to 'appen. We can 'ardly go and camp outside the bank waiting for it to arrive and see who else turns up."

"No but we could go along to the bank to discuss depositing something there and see what we can pick up, you never know there might be someone susceptible to my charms there. Your superior hearing might pick up a snippet or two."

"A trip to the bank it is, I'll break out me best suit for the occasion. Now though I think we've done enough for today, I'm for bed. I'll see you in the morning."

Polly smiled at him.

"Yes, bed sounds good, it's been an interesting day and who knows what tomorrow will bring."

4 THE BANK

Polly and Will arrived at the Whithersnick bank just after the lunch time rush. She had found in past cases that office workers were less alert just after lunch and it was easier to find out information at that time. With a final tug at his stiff collar, Will opened the door for Polly and followed her in. They were greeted by a long counter in front of them that went from one side of the room to the other. Openings showed along the counter and behind them were sat bank tellers protected from any attack by metal grills that came down to a hand's width above the counter.

"Designed against force but not the wiles of a woman," thought Will as he saw the reaction to their entrance.

Polly had chosen their disguise well as he watched the way all the bank tellers went a little dazed as they caught sight of her, then they saw him behind her and flashes of jealously spiked in their eyes.

Her hair was piled high on her head, held by pins that glittered and shone, a small dark green pillbox hat was attached at an angle and an iridescent blue and purple butterfly brooch held it secure.

She had on a purple velvet skirt with dark green ruffles and a matching green corset which had the same butterfly from her hat embroidered into the rich material. Her shirt was as white as it could possibly be and the outfit was completed by a fitted purple jacket that came down to just below the top of her corset and which was done up across at the top with bright silver buttons made to look like scarabs. Neat kitten heel black boots showed at the bottom of her skirt, whilst her hands were covered by intricate lace black gloves.

"She looks as pretty as a picture and so elegant," Will thought to himself and then concentrated on the job in hand.

Following Polly up to the first window that was available he smiled as he watched the young man behind the desk try to find the ability to speak to the vision in front of him. Polly just smiled and waited.

"Can I? …. Please may I?… How?.," the young man stumbled and tripped over his words.

"My husband and I would like to discuss opening a deposit box here, would that be possible?" Polly asked.

"A deposit box, yes, of course, I will get my manager to speak to you." The young man jumped up from his desk, bowed, turned, nearly tripped over his chair, caught himself and then hurried through a door behind him.

The sounds of hurried footsteps came to Will's superior hearing.

"So far, so good, sounds like we've got to the next step with no problem," whispered Will. Polly shot a glance to him.

"Let's wait till we get inside before we congratulate ourselves."

The door at the back opened and a middle-aged man with thinning hair and a stern expression, dressed in a smart dark grey suit came in closely followed by the young bank teller who pointed towards Polly and Will. The man came over to them and spoke to them through the grill.

"I believe you wish to open a deposit box; may I have a bit more information from yourselves. You must understand that procedure must be followed and the reputation of the bank must be preserved."

Polly smiled at him but the man did not return her smile.

"We totally understand Mr …?"

"I am Mr Able, the day Manager for this week."

"Nice to meet you Mr Able" Polly said.

"That's as maybe Miss but you still need to give me a little more information before I can ascertain whether we can help you."

Will felt Polly tense and wondered if a charm was to follow but then she smiled again.

"It's Mrs, if you don't mind, my name is Mrs Dogwood, this is my husband, Matthew. We are new to London and are in the process of buying a property and have some items of jewellery, specifically pieces left to me by my mother, that need to be kept secure whilst we set up our new home. As such we wish to talk to a few banks to learn which we feel can best meet our needs."

"What sort of value are we talking Mrs Dogwood," Mr Able said without much enthusiasm.

Polly turned to Will.

"Matthew, my dear, may I have the jewellery case?"

Will reached into his jacket pocket and pulled out a long thin box and passed it her.

"These were my mother's pearls, she also left me two diamond necklaces, one with a ruby stone and the other an emerald. There are also some matching earrings and my father's pocket watch, which whilst not as expensive as my mother's pieces holds great sentimental value to me."

She pushed the box through the grill opening and Mr Able took it and opened it. His demeanour changed immediately; pulling himself up straighter he grimaced a smile at them, closed the box and passed it back to Polly.

"I think we would certainly be able to help you Mrs Dogwood, if you would be so good as to come to the door at the end of the counter I will let you in and we shall discuss terms."

They turned and walked along to the end of the counter and reached it just as Mr Able opened the door and stood back to allow them to enter. He then took them round the room and opened the door at the back through which he had come and led them through it and into a corridor which had numerous doors leading off it. Mr Able led them to the first door and opening it, gestured for them to come in.

"Now I just need to take some information from you and then we can set up the box for you," he said as he went behind a small desk that took up most of the width of the room. Tall bookshelves full of paper and books ringed the room. Mr Able went to one pile of paper and picked up the top few sheets before turning back to Polly and Will and pointing to the chairs in front of the desk.

"Please sit down, this will take a while, there is lots of information we need to obtain."

Polly sighed and Will felt the air shimmer a little as the familiar tug of magic played on his senses.

"Mr Able, much as we would love to fill out all your forms in triplicate for you, we would much rather just have a tour of the deposit box room to assure ourselves that it is a safe place for our treasured possessions. If we are not happy with that then we can leave and not have to waste time completing your paperwork."

A slightly dazed expression came over Mr Able, he twitched as though a bee had come too close to him and then he relaxed.

"I've just had a good idea," he said, "why don't I show you the deposit box room, so that you feel safe leaving your possessions here."

"What a wonderful idea Mr Able," said Polly, nudging Will as he started to grin a little too much. "We would love you to show us that."

Mr Able went to a small safe behind the desk, turned the dial on it back and forth as the tumblers fell into place and then pulled down the handle, opened it and took out a bunch of keys.

"Please follow me" he said and led them out of the room and along the corridor to a door at the end. There was a key pad as a lock and he pushed four buttons, there was a click and the door opened onto a staircase which led down to a solid wood door which was locked by three locks. Mr Able used three keys from the set he had and then pushed the door slowly open. It opened onto a large room which would have been the cellar but now was lined at the back by shelves holding hundreds of metal boxes. In front of the shelves and dividing the room in half were metal bars, a barred door was set into the bars with a large lock and heavy hinges holding it in place.

"Here is where your box would be kept, Mrs Dogwood. There is only one key for the metal door and that is kept by Mr Whithersnick Snr himself and the door is only opened when either he or Mr Whithersnick Jnr is present. Anybody who goes into the area is accompanied by a member of our security team, that is led by Mr Belton, who is late of her Majesty's army. We believe that our security is the best there is, the first door can only be opened with the correct code, a code which changes on a weekly basis. The second door requires three keys, which are kept in the safe in the front office, the combination of which is also changed on a regular basis.

"Mr Able, your protection against intruders is impressive but what protection is there for natural disasters, say a fire broke out, would our possessions be safe?"

Mr Able smiled. "Do not fear Mrs Dogwood, the bank has the most sophisticated sprinkler system available. The system runs throughout the building, there is a main lever on the ground floor within my office, then on each floor there is a lever which will only set the sprinklers going for that area. Look, here is the one for this room, right next to the door, so if anything happened it can easily be reached."

"Thank you Mr Able for showing us this, it is much appreciated and I agree your security and protection is most impressive. We shall certainly keep your bank in mind for storing our precious items, when we arrange the transporting of them."

Mr Able led them out and up to the main floor, meticulously locking all the locks on the way out. As they walked along the corridor Polly looked in one of the other offices that had an open door and saw Terrance sitting at a desk surrounded by books piled high and a large ledger open in front of him. He looked up and gaped as he recognised her. He went to say something but then saw Mr Able and hastily went back to work.

Polly and Will allowed Mr Able to escort them into the front office of the bank and said their goodbyes to him with assurances of their return in the future, before making their way into the street.

"Let's walk a little way away Will before we confer," she said as she took his arm and they walked away.

"Good thing the Organ Grinder isn't around," said Will, "I was a bit worried that we would have to deal with a crazy monkey when we came out of the bank."

Polly stopped walking and looked around. "You're right, he's not here, I hadn't noticed. He was stood just over on that corner yesterday, now why isn't he here today I wonder?"

"Could be, cause he already knows that whatever it is in that bank they want is already in there."

"Did you see the marking on one of the boxes; it was Lord Astborough's mark?"

"But that don't make any sense Polly. If'n you reckon Lord Astborough is using Innocent to steal something he wants why 'as he got a box in there?"

Polly was about to say something when they both heard someone calling Polly's name. They turned back and saw Terrance running towards them.

"Miss Polly, you came, thank you so much, you've done it you got rid of the Organ Grinder, he isn't here today."

"A fact we were just discussing. Terrance allow me to introduce my partner, Will Dagger. Will this is Terrance Biggar."

Will put out a hand and Terrance shook it, still babbling his thanks to Polly about the lack of the Organ Grinder.

"Please Terrance, stop for a moment I need to ask you a question."

"Oh, sorry, of course, what is it?"

"The delivery you overheard being discussed, has that been made?"

"Yes, Miss Polly, a man came this morning with a box that he handed over to Mr Whithersnick Jnr with the strict instructions that it should not be opened on pain of death and should be stored upright and with great care."

"And was it put down in the secure area?"

"Yes, I saw them go down with it, why Miss Polly?"

Polly looked up at Will.

"Are you thinking what I'm thinking Will?"

"If you mean about Lord Astborough maybe wanting revenge and using someone to be his scapegoat then possibly."

Polly looked back at Terrance.

"Terrance, Will and I need to spend some time tonight in the Whithersnick Bank, will you trust us and allow us entrance after everyone has gone home for the night?"

"Why, what do you think is going to happen, I mean the Organ Grinder has gone, he can't do any harm now can he?"

"This has gone beyond a watcher at the gate, Terrance, I believe that someone wants to destroy the Whithersnick bank and I think they will attempt it tonight. Your only hope of having somewhere to come to work tomorrow is to let us in and hope that we can stop whatever is going to happen, happening."

Terrance looked at Polly as though wanting to disbelieve her but then he sighed.

"I can let you in. There is a staff entrance at the back of the building, if you are there at six o'clock this evening I can let you in as I leave but you will have to very careful that no-one sees you around that spot. I do not know where you are going to hide in the bank as Mr Belton and his security guards do walk around the bank at regular intervals throughout the night in case of intruders."

"Don't worry about us Terrance we can stay hidden and we will make sure that no-one knows that it was you that let us in."

"You really think the bank is in danger?"

"Yes Terrance I do, there is a man that only understands how to destroy and we have thwarted him once, I just hope we can do it again."

Terrance studied her and then nodded. "Very well I will see you at six o'clock."

"Thank you Terrance," Polly said and taking Will's arm again they walked away as Terrance turned and went back to work.

Just before six o'clock they were back outside the Whithersnick Bank, though this time they were both wearing dark clothing more suited for night time adventures than their morning wear.

"Do you really reckon that Lord Astborough is aiming to destroy the bank then Polly?" asked Will, as they waited for the bank staff to leave for the night.

"Let's think about what we know Will, the Organ Grinder was there as a lookout, ostensibly sent by Innocent but I think there for Lord Astborough so that he can feed Innocent with lies. The Organ Grinder tells Innocent a delivery of great wealth is going to be made, probably even describes the box it is in. Somehow Innocent gets in and past all the security men and through all the locked doors and opens the box left there by Lord Astborough. Is it jewels or gold in that box or is it something that will destroy Innocent along with anyone standing near him and bring down the bank around them? I'm betting it's the latter scenario rather than the former and I don't wish to see either Colossus or Innocent harmed just to satisfy Lord Astborough's need to bring about disaster on those that hurt his family name."

"But that box wasn't that big Polly, what could he have put in there that would hurt someone that opens it?"

"I don't know Will but hopefully we can stop it happening. Look the lights are beginning to all go out, let's make our way round to the back."

They got there just as they saw Terrance open a door and stand there looking around for them. They quickly entered and he took them along to the office Polly had seen him in earlier.

"I have to go out the front way so that the security guard sees me leave and I'm supposed to lock the office door."

"Then lock it Terrance, it will be safer for us if it is locked, a security guard is less likely to come in then," said Polly, "don't worry we have ways to get through locked doors, we will stay hidden and if nothing happens tonight we will let ourselves out without anyone knowing we were here."

Terrance looked worried but left the office, locked the door and they heard his steps disappear through into the front of the bank and his goodnight spoken to the guard.

They settled down to wait, both sitting down against the wall nearest the door.

The first time the security guard walked along the corridor, they both held their breath but after a simple try of the door handle, he had walked away and they had relaxed. Whilst there might be a good number of guards patrolling the building they had obviously become lax in their duties, trusting that a locked door meant that everything was as it should be.

Polly could feel herself beginning to fall asleep, when Will stiffened beside her.

"What is it?" she whispered.

"The guard should have come along the corridor, I thought I heard a soft thump a little while ago but wasn't sure, now he's not here. Someone else is in this bank."

Polly strained to hear but only silence greeted her. She stood up and went to go to the door to unlock it but Will stopped her.

"Someone's coming, it's not the guard, let's wait a moment, don't fire up any spells, if you're right and Colossus is out there, we don't want him being alerted to our presence."

Polly squeezed his hand in response and they stood back against the wall, hidden in the shadows.

Soft footsteps sounded along the corridor, hardly making a sound across the wooden floorboards. Two faint shadows passed by the glass panel in the door, one tall and the other even taller. Will had been correct; Mr Innocent and Colossus had got into the bank. They didn't move as they heard the footsteps move to the locked door at the end of the corridor. There was the four-step sound of buttons on the keypad being pressed and the door scraped along the floor as it was opened. Then the footsteps faded as the owners walked down the stairs.

Polly crept to the door and using a set of lock picks quickly opened the door and she and Will moved towards the end of the corridor. Thankfully Innocent had left the first door open, obviously for ease of escape with whatever he managed to steal. They stopped at the entrance and listened. From below they could hear the slight sound of scratching, which Polly recognised as someone using lock picks, just as she had, then the solid clunk as they caught and the lock opened.

"We're in."

The quiet words drifted up the staircase to Polly and Will as they heard the door being opened and the movement of the two men into the inner room. They stayed at the top of the staircase and listened as the intruders below got through the last metal barred door and into the shelving area. They could hear them moving boxes around and then the excited sound as they located the one they wanted.

Just as they could hear them lifting the box down there was the sound of the metal door shutting and clicking the lock into place.

"Get the door open Col, I'll open the box."

There was a click as Innocent did as he said, then a fizzing sound like acid burning through something, a cry of "No", a crash and an explosion echoed up the staircase and light shone up illuminating Polly and Will. Alarms began to sound all around them. She stared at Will and began to run down the stairs.

Fire was everywhere in the box room, creeping along the floor and up the wooden shelving. The box in the centre of the room was burning furiously and off to one side Innocent was struggling to get out from under Colossus who had obviously jumped in between him and the box and protected him from the worst of the explosion.

Innocent saw Polly and Will and stared at them in confusion.

"Quick Will, turn the sprinklers on," Polly said. She ran to the barred door, a bolt of power from her hand hit the lock and it disintegrated and fell away. She pulled the door open and began to make her way over to where Innocent was desperately pulling at Colossus' smouldering clothing; the smell of burnt flesh filled her senses. Colossus wasn't moving and she was terrified the explosion had already done its worst. She bent down to try and help Innocent pick up Colossus but he was too heavy for her.

"It's not working" shouted Will as he pulled on the lever Mr Able had shown them earlier. No water came out of the sprinklers and the fire continued to increase.

"Quick Will, get Colossus out, he's too heavy for me, I'll help Innocent and sort out the fire."

Will ran over to her, bent down, took hold of Colossus and dragged him over to outside of the bars. Polly followed him helping Innocent as he staggered, still dazed from the explosion.

They could still hear the cacophony of alarms sounding all around them.

"We must get out Polly, the peelers will be here soon."

"Get them both out of here Will. I must stop the fire, I cannot let the bank burn and Lord Astborough win."

Will bent down, pulled Colossus on to his shoulder and then pushed Innocent ahead of him and up the stairs.

Polly turned back to the fire and concentrated.

"Water of the heavens, rain down on me
That this fire of destruction shall burn no more

Water of the heavens, hear my plea
Enough to heal and not to flood.
As it harm none my will be done."

Droplets of water began to fall from the ceiling and sputter against the strong flames, then more water began to flow and the fire began to fall back until it disappeared completely and the box that had started it all sat blackened and full of water on the floor. Polly turned and ran up the stairs where she found Will waiting with Colossus on the floor next to him and Innocent sat against the wall.

"I thought I told you to get out," she snapped at Will and then looked at Colossus slumped on the floor, "is he?"

"He's alive, out cold though and weighs a ton. Mr Innocent there didn't think you were going to make it, wouldn't let me leave until you came out."

"Men, why do they always think I'm incapable of sorting things out? Come on Mr Innocent, it is time to leave, we are close to being caught in here and I don't think you want your reputation ruined over an abortive arson attack."

"Aren't you the perky one right about now? Is she always right?" said Innocent.

"Most times and I've found it much better to do what she says, safer that way. Come on Crime Lord, time to get to the shadows, those Peelers will be here soon."

Will picked up Colossus again as Polly helped Innocent stand up and she led the way to the entrance that Terrance had brought them in through earlier. Carefully she picked the lock and opened the door.

"Can you hear anything Will, other than the alarms?"

"The peelers are coming, I can hear their whistles but they're a fair way away yet. We've got time to disappear before they come but I can sense people are beginning to look out to see what is happening. Reckon you can pull a cover spell for all of us?"

"As long as we don't move too fast and stick together, yes I can do that."

Will led the way out of the door, carrying Colossus and stood waiting holding onto Innocent as Polly locked the door behind them. She nodded to him once the spell was in place and they carefully walked away and melted into the shadows of the dark streets.

They had only been walking a short time when Innocent stopped, looked around and said.

"Come with me, I have a safe house not two minutes from here, we can get inside and I can look to my friend."

He led them down a few more dark streets and then knocked quietly on a door. It was opened by an old man, who took one look at Innocent, nodded in greeting, turned and led them in to the house. He beckoned them to follow him along a short corridor and led them up a flight of stairs to a bedroom holding a large double bed. Will gratefully placed Colossus onto it face down and then stood stretching out his back and giving a sigh of relief.

"I'm glad you knew of this place, he was beginning to get a bit 'eavy even for me."

"What are you?" asked Innocent, "I couldn't lift him, could hardly get out from under him, yet you have just carried him the better part of a mile, how?"

"Just naturally strong I guess it's in me nature."

"You are more than naturally strong, how did you . .?"

"Let's not worry about how Will carried Colossus please Mr Innocent, rather let's see what can be done to help him."

Polly went over to the unconscious man and taking out a small knife from her pocket began to cut away the burnt clothing.

Innocent brought a lamp over and stood next to her so that she could more easily see what she was doing. The skin across Colossus' back was raw and badly burnt. His clothing had stuck to him as it burnt and cutting it away caused the skin to tear and peel.

"You ask about Will but in return I ask you about Colossus, this much damage to a normal person would kill them, yet he is still breathing," said Polly.

"He's a good healer, not invincible but he can certainly take more than most. Though I have not seen him this damaged before. He saved my life, I heard the click and the sound of the acid and then I was flying through the air and crashing against the floor with him on top of me on fire. I couldn't get out from under him and I thought we were both goners and then you arrived. Where did you come from? Why did you come? What did you think was going to happen?"

"Stop Mr Innocent, it is enough that we were there, now give me some space and I can help Colossus to heal."

She held her hands out over the ravaged skin and as she whispered words of power, cool white light danced from her fingertips and flowed across the wounds. Colossus stirred and groaned with pain as the wounds slowly pulled together, the skin turning from burnt to pinky white and then darkening to Colossus' normal tone. Polly could read across his back the tale of floggings and sword fights, here and there the puckering of a stab from a knife, now the new scars of burnt flesh would tell another story.

Polly stopped and Will caught her as she stumbled back exhausted from the effort.

"Is there another bed in this house Mr Innocent, she needs to sleep now, it's been a long night and magic is tiring."

"How did she do that, the burns are gone, I don't understand, who are you? Why would she do that? What are you?"

"Too many questions for now Mr Innocent, just accept that we are the people that got you out of a burning building, saved your reputation, black as it is and right now, Polly needs to sleep, so please a bed now."

Colossus groaned and turned his head to look at them both.

"She warned me," he whispered, his voice unsteady.

"What?" asked Innocent leaning into hear him better.

"She warned me, she told me to take care, that we might get burnt" he sighed and laughed gently "though I didn't think she meant literally. Take good care of her Inno, she saved us both tonight."

Innocent looked at him, then gently touched his shoulder, as he stood back up.

"I will look after them my friend, sleep now, we will go home tomorrow."

Colossus sighed again, "Home, yes, tomorrow".

He closed his eyes and was asleep as Innocent motioned to Will, who picked Polly up and followed him out and up another flight of stairs to a further bedroom with another double bed. Innocent pulled back the heavy quilt and Will put Polly down.

"Thank you Mr Innocent, I will see to Polly now."

"I can send the old man's wife up to help you, if you wish to someone to make her more comfortable."

Will smiled.

"There are no secrets between Polly and I, she has nursed me and I her, I will be fine."

"You have known her a long time then? Is she your … I mean are you and she …? Innocent stumbled to a halt.

"She is the one person who understands me in this world Mr Innocent, she is precious to me but I would never presume to be anything but her friend, anything else would break the magic that we have."

"What are you Will? You carried Colossus, I have had to help him stagger away from things before now and I know how heavy he is. I can hardly lift him but to walk as far as you did, I cannot understand it."

"As with Polly there is more to me than at first sight but it is not something I would choose to share with you tonight, Mr Innocent. I do not know whether I trust you yet."

"I understand, but trust this Will, Polly saved the man I consider my true brother. Col is the only man who I would lay my life down for without hesitation. I would rather cut off my own arm than have any harm come to you who have saved him. Sleep well Will, you are safe here."

"Thank you Mr Innocent. Now please I need to make Polly comfortable, there is nothing she hates worse than waking up with her boots still on."

Innocent smiled, "I will go and sit with Colossus, I have much to think on. I need to plan how to deal with those within my organisation who may not be as loyal as I would wish."

"I trust you will discover also those that are true to you. Colossus will be fine, she's a good healer, sorted me out a few times, he's got a few new scars but he'll live."

"And as I leave you hand me another mystery to consider, what were you doing to earn scars?"

"Growing up Mr Innocent. An orphanage is a tough place for those that are different.

"Different, then I guess you are in good company as I would certainly consider myself and Col as different, we sit outside the regular society of this fair city and we survive. Maybe tonight has been more than just a failed bank robbery. Maybe it will be the start of something else."

Innocent turned and left, gently closing the door behind him.

"Maybe Mr Innocent, maybe," said Will quietly as he heard Innocent head back down the stairs. He sat on the bed and gently unlaced Polly's boots and pulled them off.

Polly stirred.

"Will?" she murmured.

"Yes, Polly, it's me, go back to sleep."

"Help me get my corset off Will, it's too tight to sleep in."

She turned over on to her front and Will undid the lacing loosening it at much as he could. Polly turned back and he unhooked the front and eased the whole thing out from under her as she stretched up and took a deep breath.

"That feels better, thank you Will."

Will moved to the other side of the bed, removed his own boots and lay down beside her.

"Are we safe here Will? I didn't really take much notice of things earlier, I was too worried about Col."

"We'll be fine Polly, you've saved 'is best friend's life, I reckon you could ask for the moon right about now and he'd do 'is dammedest to get it for you."

"I doubt Lord Astborough will feel the same way. We messed up his plans again, didn't we? He won't be happy if he works out it was us."

"Shh, don't think about that now, we are safe for tonight, we will deal with consequences tomorrow."

"I'm cold, Will."

"It's using all that power, you need time to recover, come 'ere I'll keep you warm."

Polly cuddled up to Will as he pulled the covers up and over them both.

"You were always good at keeping me warm. Consequences tomorrow then, goodnight Will."

"Goodnight Polly," said Will but she was already asleep. He smiled, sighed contentedly and in seconds was sound asleep as well.

THE CASE OF TOO MANY FISH

1 THE ACCUSED

Gadget burst through the door shouting for Polly.

"What on earth are you making such a racket for?" asked Polly as she came from the small room off of the office.

"There's a massive black man downstairs, he wants our help. He's waiting downstairs, Mr Hardaker is trying to get him to buy a copper pan but I think he's scared of him. The man is covered in scars."

"Then that is Colossus and he is a friend, please tell him to come up, he is welcome in our office at any time."

Gadget ran out of the room and started shouting for Colossus to come upstairs even as she bounded down them.

"That child really does need to learn some decorum, I despair sometimes" thought Polly.

She heard Colossus' deep tones thanking Gadget and then he came up the stairs making far less noise than Gadget had. He stopped at the door and knocked at the glass panel.

Polly opened the door fully.

"Hello Col, how are you, come in, you don't have to knock and wait. It's good to see you."

She reached out and took one of his hands and pulled him into the room. Colossus had to duck to get through the doorway and then he stood looking down at her with an odd look on his face.

He was dressed in a smart suit with a stiff collar.

"You look very smart, what is the occasion?"

Colossus hesitated, looked down at Polly's hand still held in his and squeezed it gently.

"I need your help Miss Polly, I don't know who else to talk to about this. I want it done right see and Innocent he doesn't understand. He doesn't respect the law you see, so he can't see what I see."

Polly smiled up at him and led him over to the armchairs. Letting go of his hand she gestured to the chair behind him.

"Sit down Col, tell me what is wrong and if I can help of course I will."

Colossus sat down gently in the chair, his long legs pulled up in front of him as he sank back down into the soft cushions.

"You have a nice office Miss Polly, it's neat and clean, not like Innocent's office. That's a mess, paper, plates, mugs, glasses, cigar butts all over the place."

"I doubt you came here to talk about Innocent's housekeeping abilities or to ask me to help you tidy his office up, so what is wrong?"

Colossus sighed.

"No I came because I have a good friend that is in trouble. He's been arrested for murder and I think he might hang for it, unless you can find out the truth."

"Murder Col, I'm not sure why you think I can help, I don't really know how to operate in your world."

"That's the thing Miss Polly, my friend isn't like me or any of the people that I see on a daily basis. Amos Waters is a good man, he works hard, he's not a criminal Miss Polly, he's a family man, he doesn't deserve to hang for something I would swear on my life he didn't do. Amos couldn't kill anyone Miss Polly; it's just not in his nature."

"Then you had probably better tell me who your friend has been accused of murdering."

"I'd better tell you the whole story Miss Polly."

"That would help."

"Last night, Amos' wife came to the inn asking for me, she was terrified, I don't know how she managed to get through all the riff raff unscathed but she did. She told me that Amos had been arrested for killing his boss, Mr Mason, of the Mason Shipping Company but she knew he hadn't done it. Only the Peelers were certain so no-one was going to investigate on Amos' behalf, he was going to be tried for murder and hanged. I took her home and promised her I would see what I could do. Innocent thought we should just break into the prison and rescue him but then Amos would be an escaped felon. He loves his job, I know how much respect he has for Mr Mason, and he wouldn't kill him. I decided that I would see if you could help. Will you come with me to the prison, they'd let you in to talk to Amos I know they would. Can you help me find out the truth?"

Polly looked at him and smiled.

"Of course I will help, let's get Will involved as well, I wouldn't want to investigate anything without him along."

Colossus pushed himself up from the armchair. "Can we go now, I want to get in to see Amos to let him know that I've got someone to help him, he won't do well in prison, we both had enough of captivity to last us a lifetime. I need to give him hope that he will get through this, otherwise he might just give up and die before we can help."

"It's not an easy place to get into Col, we will need money."

"That I have Miss Polly and plenty of it, I would give everything I had to help Amos, he kept me alive and believed in me when a lot of other people didn't. If it wasn't for him, I wouldn't have survived long enough for Innocent to find me. I owe Amos' everything."

"Then I will do everything I can to help him, I promise. Go downstairs and talk to Will, tell him where we are going. I will get changed into something a little more appropriate for a visit to Newgate Prison."

Colossus suddenly lifted Polly up into a big hug, and then put her back down.

"I knew you would help me Miss Polly, thank you."

He disappeared out of the door; nearly knocking his head on the doorframe and she heard him hurry down the stairs.

"He'll give Mr Hardaker the fright of his life if he smiles at him" she thought as she hurried upstairs to her bedroom to search out some suitable attire.

When she came back down stairs in a smart brown skirt, corset and jacket, carrying a smart leather bag she saw Will and Colossus stood outside.

"I 'ad to send 'em outside Polly, the store ain't big enough for those two," said Mr Hardaker, "they make me feel very small, except from side to side so to speak." He looked at Polly, "sounds like you've got your work cut out on this one, you take care in that prison, it ain't a nice place to visit and it's an even worse place to be held in."

"I will Mr Hardaker, I think I'll be safe enough with Will and Col, I don't think many prison guards would be willing to take them on and Col has assured me he has enough coin to ease our path."

She left the shop and looked up at the two men waiting for her.

"Shall we go then and see what the situation is?"

"I've a cab waiting for us Miss Polly," said Col and escorted her across the road to the waiting hansom cab.

The smell of death and decay reached them before they got to the prison, they could hear the cries of prisoners being tortured and the three of them fell silent in the face of such misery and despair. The cab stopped and it was a moment before they could summon up the energy to get out. Polly looked at Col.

"Come on, the sooner we get in there, the sooner your money can help

Amos and we can see how to proceed."

Col nodded and climbed out of the cab, turning to help her down and Will joined them a second later. The cabbie didn't wait but spurred his horses to get him away from the hateful aroma.

Col led them to the main gate and knocked loudly on the door, nothing happened, so Col hammered again on the door.

They heard a shuffling sound from inside and a grunted "alright, I'm a coming."

Then the door was unlocked and opened to show them a round rough looking man. He looked up at Col and took a step back and went to shut the door in their face but Polly stepped forward, placed her hand on the door and smiled at the man.

"Please Sir, we are here to visit a prisoner, brought in yesterday, we have money to help his stay in your establishment to be eased."

The man looked suspiciously at her.

"It ain't my establishment and you got to see the Governor if'n you want to see a prisoner. Who are you?"

"My name is Miss Baker; this is Master Dagger and Master Col. We are part of the Baker & Dagger Investigating team and are here to prevent a miscarriage of justice."

"Don't tell me, the prisoner you've come to see is innocent," he leered at her, "didn't you know Miss Baker, they's all innocent in 'ere." The man laughed and turned away, gesturing for them to follow him. He led them through a stone corridor up some stairs to a door at the top, where he knocked and on a command to enter, opened the door and led the three in.

The man sitting opposite them at a broad oak desk was in a smart black suit, with a pair of spectacles perched on the end of his nose. His hair was grey and cut short to his head and a scar cut through one eyebrow to give him a permanent look of enquiry on his face.

"Yes, Master Billings, what is it?"

"These three 'ere would like to visit a prisoner Sir, seems they feel 'e is innocent" and with that the man exited chuckling to himself.

The Governor stood up from his desk, which didn't help much as he was far shorter than either Will or Col but Polly guessed it made him feel slightly better. He walked over to the window behind him and looked down over the courtyard below.

"There are nearly 100 prisoners down there, men, women and children; over half of them will tell you they haven't done anything wrong, they are innocent. I have never believed one of them. Who is it you wish to see and what is he accused of?"

Polly stepped forward.

"His name is Amos Waters and he is accused of the murder of Mr Mason of the Mason Shipping Company."

The Governor turned to look at them, he took his glasses off, took a clean handkerchief out of his waistcoat pocket, methodically cleaned the lenses before carefully folding the handkerchief and placing it back in his pocket. He replaced his glasses on his head and peered at his three visitors.

"Well you don't look mad but I am as certain as I can be that you are. Amos Waters was found standing over the dead body of his employer with the murder weapon in his hand covered in blood. That's about as an obvious proof of crime as I can think. There's men out there convicted with less."

"Yet we believe he is innocent and would like to speak to him if that was possible?"

The Governor pondered them for a little longer but then went to the wall and pulled on a bell rope. His summons was answered in a short space of time by a sturdy looking man wearing a uniform that held on a belt a short thick baton and a bunch of keys.

"Please escort these three to the visitors' room and arrange for Amos Waters to be brought to them. They believe him to be innocent."

The man smiled a crooked smile, bowed to the Governor and gestured for the three to follow him. He led them back through the stone corridors to a room that had one window on the outside wall, heavily barred with no way of opening it to get any fresh air into the room. A desk and one chair, no other furniture was in the room.

The man left them there with an order to not attempt to leave the room and disappeared out of sight.

Will shook his head, "I do not like this place, there are corpses in this prison I can smell them. If we manage to get out of here without catching the plague I'll go to church to say a prayer of thanks."

"Be quiet Will, have some care. Col's friend is stuck here unless we can do something to find out what happened."

"Sorry Col, I didn't mean any harm."

"It's alright Will; I can't say I'm enjoying this much myself. It's taking everything I've got to not try to rip those bars away from the window and jump out and get away myself."

"Someone's coming, I can hear chains clanking," said Polly.

The three waited and then the guard came in the room followed by a small black man shackled by large leg and wrist irons. He seemed weighed down and already half way dead to Polly, she gasped and went over to him, gently took his arm and led him to the chair to sit down.

Col stalked over to the guard and took out a roll of money from an inner pocket of his jacket. The man looked at it and smiled thinly. Peeling a note off Col passed it the guard.

"Take those irons off him."

The guard looked at the note in front of him.

"I'll take 'em off for that but it'll take more to keep 'em off."

Col's muscles tightened and his face hardened, the atmosphere in the room suddenly seemed electric and Polly was sure that he was about to erupt in the violence he was desperately trying to keep in check. Then he forcefully relaxed, peeled off a large number of notes from his roll and handed them to the guard.

"There is enough there to keep the irons off of him and for him to be in a cell of his own with food and water provided and a blanket to sleep in. I will return tomorrow and if I find out that this has not been done I will seek retribution. Do you understand? I take it you have a home to go to each evening?"

The guard tried to stand up to Col's anger but could not compete with the sheer power of the big man. He gulped, nodded and snatched the money out of Col's hand. He moved past Col and bent down to remove the irons from Amos' wrists and ankles. He then went back to the door and looked at Col.

"He'll be well looked after; don't you worry none. Got to keep him good for the 'angman's noose in any case. That's where he's 'eaded and all your money won't keep 'im from it."

With that he slammed the door shut and they heard him turn the lock and leave.

"What an odious man," said Polly.

"I might seek him out one dark night and give him a bit of talking to," said Will.

Col sighed and turned to look at Amos. The man had hardly acknowledged the three of them, his head had stayed bowed and he shook with cold and hunger.

Polly reached into her bag and pulled out a sandwich and apple.

"Here," she said, "I thought you might want some food," she looked at Will and he handed over a hip flask. "There is also some brandy for you." She put the items on the table and crouched down to look up at Amos.

"My name is Polly, I'm here to help you, Col brought us. Please let me look at your wrists I can help."

The man looked dazed and confused but he held his hands out to Polly, she took them and winced at the sight of the torn skin where the irons restraints had bitten in and cut him. She let her power seep out to ease the pain and mend the cuts.

Amos looked at her in amazement and tears began to silently run down his face. Col came over to the table and leant down towards him.

"Amos, take a drink, eat some food, we need to speak to you. Polly and Will are investigators; they can help me find out what really happened. I'm sure we'll be able to prove your innocence."

Amos looked up at him and shook his head.

"No, my friend, nothing can save me now. I am bound for the hangman's noose."

Col stood up and stalked over the window; he took hold of two of the bars and pulled. Slowly they bent and buckled as he poured his strength into them. He let go and turned back to look at his friend.

"Amos, you are the one man who taught me never to give up, to keep fighting whatever the odds. I would never have survived the sea journey, my time in the pits, if you had not shown me how to fight. You cannot now give up without a struggle. Tell us what happened and let us help."

Polly stood up from healing Amos' ankles and looked at him.

"Amos, Col has told me about you, he cannot believe that you would murder your employer. Will and I are good investigators, we will find the truth if you let us. What can you lose by telling us what happened?"

"What can I lose? No it is not what I can lose that I am afraid of, it is what you will give me that scares me."

"I don't understand."

"I do not wish to be given hope, I am in Newgate Prison, amongst the dead, the dying and the desperate, hope is a dangerous commodity in a prison."

Col swore viciously.

"Then do not hope Amos, believe instead. If Polly and Will cannot get you out of here by proving your innocence be assured that I will get you out of here and away from this country if necessary, there is nothing and no one that can stand in my way," he said.

Amos looked at him and then looked over to the two bent bars in the window frame and smiled.

"You have not changed my friend; it is good to see you. Very well I will believe that you will rescue me from this hellhole and see me safe home. What is it you wish to know?"

He looked down at his wrists. "Thank you, I don't know how you did that but thank you," he picked up the sandwich, "thank you for this as well, I have had nothing since they brought me here yesterday morning."

He bit into the sandwich and groaned with pleasure. As he swallowed, he reached for the hipflask and took a long drink.

"I will tell you what little I know. Yesterday morning I got up, said goodbye to my wife and children and went along to work as usual. I went up to Mr Mason's office, went in and found him lying there on the ground with a letter opener in his chest. I ran over to him, tried to see if he was still alive, then took the letter opener and pulled it out, stupid I know but it just looked so wrong but in doing that I got blood on my hands. The next thing I know, Mr Mason's housekeeper comes in the room, the peelers are called and I'm arrested for Mr Mason's murder. Nothing I said would convince them that I had simply found him like that. I begged them to let my wife know what had happened but I had no faith that they had."

"Somebody told her, because she came to find me last night."

"Oh I married a wonderful woman, to venture to where you live, a wonderful woman."

Polly looked at him and smiled.

"It is not a lot to go on but Will and I have started cases with less, so we will get started. Will can you pound on the door let them know we wish to leave. Col are you coming with us?"

"No, I'll stay here with Amos for a while, I think I will order some food to be brought in and we can chat for a while."

The guard arrived in answer to Will's knocking and unlocked the door. Polly explained that she and Will would be leaving and Col would be staying. The guard looked a little disgruntled but led them out of the room, locking it again and then leading them down the corridor.

They had only taken a few steps when they saw a man coming towards them.

"Oh bleeding 'ell, it's Quinn what does he want?" grumbled the guard under his breath. The man stopped in front of them and look inquisitively at them.

"Hello and who are you and who have you been visiting?" he asked.

Polly looked at him, he was a wiry looking man, around forty or so she guessed, his hair had gone grey and he had it cut short. His face looked weather beaten and lined but there was intelligence behind his eyes and a quick manner about his movements that spoke of humour and curiosity.

"This 'ere is Miss Baker and Master Dagger who 'ave just been visiting Amos Waters on account of 'im being innocent," sneered the guard.

"Would that be Miss Baker and Master Dagger of Baker & Dagger Investigators?" asked the man.

"Yes" said Polly surprised that he knew who they were, "our services have been engaged by a friend of Amos Waters to prove his innocence. And if you don't mind my asking, who are you?"

The man smiled, held his hand out in greeting and whilst shaking hers he said "the name is Detective Alec Quinn and if you have been engaged in the case of Mr Waters then I need to talk to you," he turned to the guard "I will escort these two out, you can carry on with whatever mistreatment you were detained from," he looked back at Polly "please will you follow me, we have lots to discuss."

He led them out through the stone corridors until they reached the street where he hailed a cab and invited them to join him. Once on the move he said "Thank you for giving me some time, the reason I would like to talk to you is that I am also of the opinion that Amos Waters is innocent but not one of my superiors in the police will entertain the thought, so I am forced to investigate on my own. Now what I have heard about you is that you have specialist skills which assist you in your work, I could do with some specialist help."

"Would you mind if I asked you a question" said Polly.

"Of course not, ask away, my dear lady."

"Where are we going?"

"Oh, I'm sorry, how obtuse of me, I thought it might help if I took you to the crime scene. Well actually we are going to where the body and the accused was discovered. Any further information I hope you don't mind but I will keep to myself at the moment, just so that you can come to the situation clear of any preconceived ideas."

"Then we shall wait and see what we can find out for you," said Polly with a smile.

2 THE VICTIM

The cabbie pulled his horses to a standstill outside a large house not far from the docks. Black curtains hung in the windows and there was a black wreath on the front door.

Quinn jumped down, thanked the cabbie and waited for Polly and Will to join him.

"Now I don't actually have any right to walk into the house and have a look at the room where Mr Mason was found so we will have to tread carefully."

He went up to the door and gently tapped the heavy brass knocker and stepped back. They waited for a short while then the door was opened by a young girl in a plain black dress with white apron. She looked as though she had been crying but smiled when she saw Quinn.

"Good morning Detective Quinn. How can I help?"

"Good morning Maddie, how are you today?"

"I don't know Detective, we are all still here and keeping the house clean but we don't know what is going to happen when Mr Mason's son takes over, he may well not want any of us anymore."

"Please tell me no one has gone into Mr Mason's office since yesterday?"

"No, Detective, we have not wanted to and kept in mind that you asked us not to. Thankfully Mr Mason's son has not been here, we would not have been able to say no to him."

"Good, good, right then, if you don't mind I would like to show my colleagues here Mr Mason's office, I'm hoping to find out more about what happened to him."

The young girl curtsied, opened the door fully and led them through a large hallway, up a flight of stairs and stopped outside a closed door.

Quinn gently touched her arm.

"Thank you Maddie, we can take it from here, there is no need for you to see the room again."

The young girl curtsied again and then ran away from them and they could hear her crying as she ran.

"Mr Mason was well liked by his staff then?" Will asked.

"Mr Mason was well liked by everyone, except for one, who it seems disliked him intensely. Shall we go in; I would be interested to see what you discover."

Quinn opened the door and let them walk in. Polly went in first and looked around at the room. It was at the back of the house as she could see the courtyard outside through a window that stretched across the room at the back. In front of it was a heavy oak desk, its legs carved to look like dolphins leaping up out of the sea. She walked over to it and walked around to look at the chair behind it, the theme of the sea continued in the solid chair, carvings in the back panel showed a fleet of ships at sea.

Along the wall opposite the door there was a large fireplace, the fireguard in front of it was painted with another sea theme, a storm and a wrecked ship stranded against rocks. Sailors were shown struggling to stay afloat in the water, some were already sinking under the waves and others were clinging to life boats as they desperately rowed to escape the stricken vessel.

"Cheerful" said Will, he sniffed the empty grate, "something was burnt in here and recently." He looked at Quinn "did you find any scraps of paper to see what was burnt?"

"No" said Quinn.

Will went over to the coat rack, there were three coats hung on the hooks attached to the wall, he turned to Quinn.

"Are these all belonging to Mr Mason?"

"Yes" said Quinn.

Will sniffed at the coats; two were neatly arranged on the hooks, whereas the last was flung on the remaining hook.

"Odd" said Will.

"What is?" asked Quinn.

Will didn't answer but went over to the desk and sat down in the chair and touched the desk and chair. Then he got up and went to the front of the desk and knelt down on the floor sniffing at the rug which went up to meet the table legs.

"Hmm" he said as he knelt back up and looked at Polly. "I think I know who killed Mr Mason, I just don't know why."

She nodded in agreement, "yes, a little obvious I guess but what is the motive?"

Quinn coughed, "Would you mind awfully sharing your conclusions with me?"

Polly looked at him and smiled. "I'm sorry, we're used to how we think, we have a shorthand way of communicating sometimes."

She went over to the fireplace and looked down at the small pile of ash left in there.

"Would you mind if I asked you a question Detective Quinn?"

"No, please go ahead?"

"You said you needed our specialist skills because you believed that Amos Waters was innocent. What makes you believe in his innocence?"

"You will need to understand something about me; I'm an oddity within the police organisation. There are only a few of us, being a Detective is a novelty to start with and I'm a Detective that actually likes detecting, not accepting what is presented at face value. However, there must be three things that nudge my brain before I will start detecting."

"So there were three things that felt wrong with the scenario here?"

"Yes. Three things, each one on its own meaning very little but put together they tell a very different story. I'll start with the obvious, the body of Mr Mason. The housekeeper said she came in and found Amos holding the letter opener with blood on his hands. Look at the rug, where's the blood? If Amos had just stabbed Mr Mason and removed the letter opener from the wound, blood should have been all over that rug, instead there was only some on his hands. Ergo Mr Mason was already dead when the letter opener was put into his chest."

Will nodded in agreement.

"And the next two?" asked Polly.

"The second is connected to the third. You see the last coat on the rack, look at the other two, neatly hung up, those coats won't be harmed by being hung there but the last one is flung on the hook, doesn't sit right in my head."

He went over to the coat and pulled it open to show them the back of it.

"There are fish scales on the back of this coat, how did they get on the back of this coat, other than by having the coat lying on some fish for some time. I don't see any fish in this office."

"So your theory is that Mr Mason was killed somewhere else, laid down on a rack of fish before being moved to this room where the letter opener was pushed into his chest awaiting a scapegoat who would pull it out and be caught red handed. Do you have any idea who the true miscreant is?" asked Polly.

"I have a theory but I would be interested to see if you have any idea."

Polly looked at Will.

"Mr Mason has a son, right?" said Will.

"Yes" said Quinn

"That maid, Maddie, she said the son hadn't been here since the murder, had he been here before that?"

Quinn smiled.

"No, according to the housekeeper when I spoke to her yesterday after Amos had been taken away, the son and father have not been getting on very well recently and the son was not welcome in this house."

"Well he's been here and recently, I can sense familial links in scent, Mr Mason is the strongest in this room but there was another from his family in here and as recently as last night."

"So the son killed the father, a rather predictable conclusion, the only problem is proving it," said Polly, going over to the fireplace. "Whatever was burnt here, was burnt last night, could be your motive Detective Quinn."

"Could indeed be, however, all that is in that grate is ash, not one scrap of paper to give me a clue as to content survived."

Polly smiled, "time for my specialist skill to show itself I guess."

She knelt down, moved the fireguard out of the way, put her hands out and whispered. Slowly the ash rose up from the grate, swirled in front of her and then slowly in front of her, joined together in a gossamer web creating a large piece of paper, gold worlds showed against the grey.

Quinn leant in eagerly to read what was written.

"The last will and testament of Mr Michael Moses Mason . . . . . all parts of my business to Amos Waters, Henry Freeman and George Wright. This doesn't make sense."

"Keep reading I can't hold this for much longer," said Polly urgently.

"blah, blah and in so doing I disown my son and refuse him entry to any part of my business for now and for the rest of his life."

The page shivered, the words disappeared and the ash floated back down into the grate.

"Well, well, well," said Quinn "the plot thickens, the obvious question is why would Amos kill his employer and burn a will that gave the business to him? However, if you were a son that found out your father was going to disown you and make a new will to pass the business to his employees; wouldn't you want to do something about it? However in burning that piece of paper you take away any motive for Amos to commit the murder. If there is an earlier will giving the son the business then we have our motive."

"But no judge will listen to our proof, Detective Quinn, Will's nose and my page of ash, won't stand up in any court."

"It doesn't matter, my dear, I know that Amos didn't kill Mr Mason, that is enough for me to go hunting the real perpetrator and I will find the proof I need. If you were amenable to it I would be glad of your continued help."

"Of course, we promised Amos we would do all we could to help him, where you go Detective Quinn, we go."

Quinn led them back downstairs where they found Maddie waiting.

"Did you find anything Detective Quinn?" she asked.

"Maybe Maddie, we have more investigations to make though before we can prove what really happened. Thank you for letting us see the room."

"Mr Mason was a good man Detective and so is Amos, none of us believe that he could have done this, please find out who killed Mr Mason."

"I will Maddie, I promise."

Quinn led Polly and Will out of the house and stood for a moment after Maddie had shut the door. He looked ruefully at them.

"Not the best promise to make, I hope you prove me right."

"Us" said Polly, "we didn't just promise to find the killer and get him to confess, you are banking rather a lot on our skill set."

"And on myself, I know but I'm a strong believer that if you are positive you are going to find the truth then you normally do. As long as the truth turns out to be what you wish it to be all is good. Right onto the docks I think, time to talk to the other partners Henry and George. Hopefully they will have information that will help. It is not far, are you happy to walk?"

"After being in the prison earlier a walk would be good, even if the air isn't that fresh at least we are out in it," said Will. "Lead on Detective."

Quinn turned and led them along the road and then down another main road which eventually led them down to the docks, where the smell of the river mixed with the grime of the workers and the cargo they were lifting down from ships docked in the different ports.

"The Mason Shipping Company is based at the end of this dock," Quinn explained. "I spent yesterday afternoon going over his business dealings and looking at his company. It has over the years transported many things but give Mr Mason his due, he survived on legal and good moral trading. No slaves or drugs on his ships. He has employed the same workers for years, sons and fathers together. The three men, Amos, Henry and George were child slaves; he bought them and gave them their freedom, taught them the business and eventually made them partners. Do you honestly believe that one of those men would kill him?"

"Doesn't sound very likely but you know how feelings run deep with some people in positions of authority, the black man can be considered little more than an animal by some of them, incapable of loyalty or decency. The world is changing but slowly," said Polly.

Dockers on the ships stopped and watched as the trio walked by, a few wolf whistles and lewd comments came their way of how some of the men would like to treat Polly, Will growled in annoyance but Polly just smiled.

"Come on Will, they are just looking to get a reaction out of me, I don't think we need to show them our cards do you?"

"Can't you just tip a couple of them into the river; let a bale fall on their head or something."

Polly laughed and took his arm. "Let them have their fun Will, it is a hard life they lead, let them be."

Quinn stopped outside a large warehouse which had the name Mason Shipping Company emblazoned across a wide entrance.

"We're here, shall we go in and see who we can find. I'm hoping we don't meet the son, at least not yet. I want to be able to talk to Henry and George first."

A young lad came running out of the warehouse and stopped in surprise at seeing them. Quinn beckoned him over.

"My name is Detective Quinn, I want to talk to either Henry or George are they around? Have you seen Mr Mason's son this morning? Do you know where he is?"

The boy gulped and looked back into the warehouse.

"Mr Mason is at the other end of the warehouse, he's sent me to get some men to help him, if I don't run I'll be in trouble, please Mister, let me go."

"Just let me know if I can get in to see Henry or George without Mr Mason seeing me."

"If'n you go in and go right and along to the back, you'll get to the office, Henry's in there but please take care if Mr Mason sees you going there he'll make trouble for Henry."

"We'll be careful, thank you."

Quinn watched the boy run off.

"Seems Mr Mason Jnr is not that popular a man. Let us see what Henry can tell us."

Without waiting for an answer he walked up to the entrance and turned right to go along a high line of crates stacked up. Polly and Will followed after him.

"Can you locate Mr Mason's son and warn us if he is coming nearer," Polly said to Will.

He nodded, "yes I've picked up where he is, don't worry I'll keep watch as it were."

They caught up with Quinn as he got to the end of the warehouse and turned left; a corridor had been created between the wall of the warehouse and crates piled as high as could be achieved. Polly saw hundreds of bales of material stacked together, a riotous mix of colours and textiles. One column cotton weave, the next silk and then velvet and then back to cotton.

They made their way along until they saw an office space created from putting up sheets of wood to cordon off an area that held filing cabinets and a desk. One man was sitting at the desk with his head in his hands.

Quinn walked up to the doorway and knocked on the wood to attract the man's attention. He looked up and then stared at them.

"I'm sorry, who are you and what are you doing here? You do know that you shouldn't be wandering around here without a guide, it isn't safe."

"I'm sorry but we didn't want to be officially announced. Are you Henry Freeman?"

"Yes I am. Who are you?"

"Detective Alec Quinn, this is Miss Pollyanne Baker and Master William Dagger, we are here to help Amos."

The man got up from the table and came round to them and took Alec's hand and almost dragged him into the office.

"Then you are most welcome Sir, please come in all you, please sit and ask me what you will, for Amos is innocent of what he is accused of that I am certain."

Polly followed Quinn in the office as Will took up his place at the entrance, his attention focused on where Mr Mason's son was.

"I'll stay out here, keep watch to make sure that you are not disturbed," he said.

Quinn nodded his thanks to Will as he offered Polly a chair near Henry's desk.

"Henry, I need you tell me what you know about what could have caused the death of Mr Mason. We are pretty certain we know who did but we don't have any proof or an understanding of why it happened now."

Henry sat down behind the desk and looked at Quinn.

"It's because Mr Mason found out about the extra cargo his son was bringing in and he didn't approve of it. I hope you don't mind but I will have to go into a bit of history to explain how Mr Mason operated and his dealings with his son and Amos, George and myself."

"Please tell us everything you think will help."

3 THE PARTNERS

"I will need to start a long time ago, when Mr Mason was still a young man with a small child to support. He had inherited the Mason Shipping Company from his father and saw that he would need to increase the amount of stock that he could ship. However he was a very moral young man and decided that he would endeavour in all things to run a company that did not deal in the misery of human beings.

He knew that he would need assistance in the company, men who could keep records for him, understand the figures that would need to be kept to show his incomes and outgoings. He bought Amos, Henry and myself, he came down to the market and talked to us. I doubt you can imagine that Detective Quinn, we were lost, shipped half way round the world crammed into foul smelling ships, brought up into a world full of white people, who looked at us as we were nothing more than pack animals. And then a man comes up to us, sits down next to us and speaks to us in various languages until we understand what he is saying. He asked us if we understood book keeping, figures, counting and record keeping and if we didn't were we willing to learn. I said I had counted the days we had spent on the ship, I knew how old I was, I could count the stars in the sky, I told him we could all write our names, that we had survived the horrors together and did not wish to be parted.

He smiled as us and said quietly, then I must take all three of you, let us see if we can get you out of this hellhole.

He went over and he paid for us, he bought us Detective Quinn, he bought slaves to work for him. We dared to hope that he would be a good Master, hadn't he just spoken to us in our own language?"

"It seems your hopes were granted," said Quinn.

"Beyond anything we could imagine, he instructed the slave master to take off our leg irons and shackles, he reached down and helped each of us to stand. He gave us water and asked our names. He smiled at us and said, let's get away from here, we have much to discuss which should not be in the hearing of those that are the dregs of humanity.

"He took us to his home, he introduced us to his wife who showed us such kindness, there were baths ready for us to wash in, clothes laid out for us to put on and she smiled at us, told us that food was prepared for when we were washed and dressed.

I admit I cried then, I looked at Henry and George and we were all overwhelmed with gratitude.

That was the first night, the next morning, Mr Mason sat us down, told us that he needed partners in his business. He wanted to find men who could understand business and who would work with him to create a family business, one that was built on friendship and loyalty and not bought through fear and hatred.

He offered us a fair wage; he offered to train us, to teach us English to be a part of his world if we wanted it and he gave us our freedom.

Amos asked him what would happen if we didn't want it. He just pointed to the paper he had signed giving us our freedom. Then you are free to go and make your way yourself, I will provide you with a small monetary stake if you wish it. I have no desire to force you to stay here and work with me, I wish you to do it freely."

"Rather an impressive man," said Polly, "not many men would be that strong in character."

"We stayed, we learnt and we helped him create a shipping company that stands alongside the best out there but then his son grew up and wanted to learn the business. Mr Mason sent him off to sea to travel with his ships to see the other countries that we traded with, he came back full of ideas and an arrogance that his father did not understand. But Mr Mason was at heart a canny man; you do not build up a company such as this without giving yourself backup on all things.

One thing that Mr Mason never told his son was that he did everything twice. So not one person counted all the bales off of a ship but two people did. Mr Mason appointed a ships clerk to keep the books and then told George to keep his own books, secretly so that Mr Mason could whenever he desired compare the books. That way no one could steal from him."

"I take it then, he caught his son out in a lie?" said Quinn.

"Yes, you see when John Mason came home he took over the task of counting the crates in and keeping the record of them but never realised that George was doing the same thing. Then when Mr Mason checked the books he saw that there were too many fish, not once but consistently over a six-month period. George's records showed four or five more crates of fish than John's did."

"Did Mr Mason ask his son about this?"

"Not at first, because we could never find the crates you see, the only evidence we had was on paper. Without proof of what his son was doing with the extra fish he did not feel he could say anything."

"What changed?"

Will popped his head round the door.

"Someone's coming but it's not the son. I reckon it could be George."

Henry got up to look and then disappeared round a corner in the crates to emerge a few moments later with another man of similar age. He brought him into the small office and introduced him to Quinn and Polly as indeed George.

"I've told them everything up until last week; can you tell them the rest?"

"Reckon I can" George replied. "Thing is see we finally found out what John was doing. Seems he was bringing in opium in the extra crates of fish, he knew his father wouldn't approve that's why he was hiding it."

"How did you find out?" asked Quinn.

"Going round the warehouse late one night after one of our ships had come back. John had already gone out for the evening and so Mr Mason and me we went on a hunt and found a small bag that contained a block of opium. Mr Mason swore me to secrecy about it, said it wasn't enough to talk to his son about but that he would think on the situation.

The next time he spoke about it was two days ago, when he summoned us all to witness a new will that he had made, giving the Mason Shipping Company to us and disowning his son."

"We've in a way seen that will, it was burnt though, there's not enough left to prove it existed," said Quinn.

George and Henry looked at each other.

"You've forgotten what I said about Mr Mason, he always did things twice. There is another copy of the will but if we produce it, it gives Amos a motive for killing Mr Mason, it was only made a day before Mr Mason was killed."

Quinn looked thoughtful, and then asked, "was there a previous will?"

"Yes," said George, "it left everything to his son."

"Then that's motive, isn't it?" asked Polly.

"Yes," said Quinn, "but still it's not enough proof to pull John Mason in for murder."

Will popped his head round the door again.

"Mr Mason Jnr is on his way over here and I don't think he's in a very good mood."

Quinn looked at Henry, "is there somewhere we can go that he won't see us, I would like to be able to spend some time searching the warehouse."

Henry nodded, "George take them out the back way, John won't go out there, if your man out there is right Detective Quinn, John will be looking to get away for the evening, he does not like working a full day."

George led Polly and Quinn out the office and turned down the corridor and led them to a small door at the back of the warehouse, he unlocked it and took them outside, locking the door behind him.

"If we walk along to the end we should avoid John, I think that his father suspected that he started bringing opium in to sell and for his own use. His behaviour has certainly become a little erratic recently. Please follow me and we will soon have the warehouse to ourselves for you to search in. What is it you hope to find?"

"Where Mr Mason was killed," said Quinn.

"But I thought he was killed in his office?" said George.

"Oh he ended up in his office but he wasn't killed there."

George led them along the back of the warehouse and turned when they got to the end and they walked back towards the river. He gestured for them to wait whilst he walked back round to the front but then quickly came back to them.

"John's gone, Henry just waved to me that the warehouse is empty, you can search wherever you want," he said.

"Thank you George, if you don't mind we would rather do this without any onlookers," said Quinn.

"I will go and be in the office with Henry, please come and tell us if you find anything that will help Amos."

"I promise," said Quinn.

George left them and walked away down towards the office and Quinn looked at Will.

"Now how good are you at finding murder scenes?"

"George said they found opium at the back of the warehouse, I think that could be the best place to start. I'll just have to spend some time filtering out the smell of George and Henry to find John Mason and see where he has been recently."

Will walked into the warehouse and began to walk between the piled crates sniffing the air. He moved quite quickly back and forth picking up the scent trails of the different people they had encountered.

"Ah," he exclaimed, "got you, this way."

He led them down one corridor and then branched out to a small area and looked at a pile of crates that looked empty.

"Now those crates had fish in them yesterday and somewhere round here I can smell blood, human blood, so if we can have a search of the area we might find something. Got your lamp Polly, it's pretty dark under these crates."

Polly took her lamp out of her bag and passed it over to Will who crouched down and shone it under the stacked crates. He crawled around the area for a bit, then putting the lamp down so that he could see the space underneath, he took a handkerchief out of his pocket, laid down on the floor and reached under one to pull out a long thin metal spike, which he held carefully at one end by using the handkerchief.

"I think I found your murder weapon, Detective Quinn, want to see if John Mason's fingerprint is on it."

Quinn looked at him curiously.

"What are you talking about Will?"

"It's something we've been playing with; it helps to have an inquisitive child as part of the team. She had us all coating our fingers in printing ink a while ago to show us how all our fingerprints were different," said Polly

"Yes I know we all have different fingerprints but how do you reckon to see the print on there?"

"I supposed technically we don't have to, if we are sure that John Mason killed his father with that spike we just have to make him believe we can," said Polly.

"'old on to it for a moment Polly, I reckon there's more this spot can tell us," said Will as he passed over the spike. He went up to the crates and sniffed them.

"Thing is see, these two crates over 'ere, right now this lot are empty but the floor's wet around 'em and I reckon last night they was full of ice and fish. So suppose Mr Mason argued with his son 'ere last night. Say he found 'im, gutting the fish to get the opium out and in the argument he stabbed him with it, panicked and threw 'is father's body on top of the fish and ice, so that it stayed cold. Then when everyone was asleep he moved 'im up to 'is office where he laid 'im out and used the letter opener to 'ide the mark made by the spike."

"Good thinking Will," said Quinn, "it makes sense, equally it would explain the state of the body, maybe putting it on the ice stopped it seizing up the way I would have expected it too, when I thought that he had died elsewhere."

"This is all very well" said Polly, "but how do we prove that John Mason killed his father and that Amos is innocent. I don't really think that a spike covered in blood and a wet patch on a warehouse floor is going to change anybody's mind."

"Didn't George say that John was using opium as well as dealing in it?" asked Quinn.

"Yes he did, why?"

"I think I know what we can do, if he's a user, he will need it on a regular basis so if we ask him to come into the Prison as we need to discuss Amos' situation with him and we just keep him there a little too long, he will begin to suffer, maybe we can catch him out in a lie and get him to admit killing his father."

"It's possible," said Polly "that prison's a pretty horrible place, it could well affect him and confuse him into confessing."

"I have an idea of how to play it but we can't do anything until tomorrow morning. Would you be available to help? We would have to get him there early, pull him out of bed; I doubt he will have had much sleep if he has gone out to an opium den."

"We'll be there, Detective Quinn."

He smiled at both them.

"Thank you so much for your help today, I'm very glad to have made your acquaintance. Let's go back, tell Henry and George what we have found and what we hope to do, then get on home and regroup at the prison at early tomorrow morning."

4 THE SON

Polly and Will presented themselves to the Governor of Newgate Prison at eight the following morning. He was not in the best of moods, himself looking as though he had not slept well.

"I don't know why Detective Quinn wants to bother himself with this matter. We have the miscreant in our grasp; this theatrical play against the son of a respected shipping man is ridiculous."

"Not if the said son committed the crime and not Amos," said Polly, "and surely you have some misgivings otherwise you would not have agreed to the plan."

The Governor looked at her and smiled sardonically.

"Be thankful your friend has deep pockets, otherwise I would still be in my bed and enjoying myself."

Will touched Polly's sleeve as he saw her begin to reply. She looked up at him and acknowledged his touch, she shrugged, maybe her inclination to turn the Governor into a donkey for a bit wasn't the best idea if they wanted his help.

The door opened behind them and Quinn entered.

"Ah, good you are here; John Mason is now uncomfortably sat in one of the visiting rooms, looking very much the worse for wear. I have a feeling that he will soon be a lot worse off as he comes down from whatever drugs he took last night. The perfect time to catch him out I think. Are you ready Governor, I am relying on your testament when we do find out the truth. I will need you to confirm what has gone on as you are the unbiased member of the audience."

The Governor gave a grunt and then said, "Let's go and get it over with, I am tired today and not in the mood for your games." He walked round them and went out of the door.

Quinn turned to Will, "now there will come a point and I really hope you are good at timing things, because I will need you to come in and announce that you have found the will, with any luck John Mason will fold and admit the truth at that point. If not, I hope Miss Polly that you have something up your sleeve that could get him to admit the truth without it seeming too much of a stretch for our Governor to accept. Do you get my meaning?"

"I will do what I can Quinn, do not fear," she said, "I don't think it would be wise to keep the Governor waiting, shall we follow him?"

Quinn nodded and held the door open for them to exit and he followed afterwards. They caught the Governor up and the four of them went back to the room they had first met Amos in the day before. The Governor, Polly and Quinn entered the room and Will stayed outside, out of sight of the man sitting at the table in the room.

John Mason looked tired and worn out, his eyes were bloodshot and his clothing was creased and dirty. There was in his bone structure a shadow of the man that Polly imagined his father would have been but there was a looseness to the skin and a sallow cast to his colouring that spoke of misuse and regular drug taking. He was holding his hands tight together in his lap but Polly could see tremors pulsing through his fingers. He was not in a good state and it didn't look like he was going to get better any time soon.

He looked up at Quinn and sneered.

"What is the meaning of this Detective, why did you need to see me at this ungodly hour, you have the murdering swine that killed my father, what do you need to talk to me about?"

Quinn smiled and sat down at the table opposite John Mason, he gestured to the Governor to sit next to him and Polly went over to the corner and sat down herself.

"I really appreciate you coming in Mr Mason and if it were not for tight deadlines that the Governor has to follow in dealing with Amos Waters today we would not have bothered you at all. But there are just a few questions that still need answering in regard to Mr Waters' guilt, to ensure that we all do our God given duty correctly. It would be a bad thing to send an innocent man to the gallows Mr Mason; we need to be satisfied that we have done the right thing."

"Of course he's guilty, wasn't he found standing over my father with the murder weapon in his hand. What more proof do you need?"

"Ah yes but you see what concerns me and the Governor here," Quinn looked at the man sat next to him, who really didn't look concerned but Quinn carried on regardless "our concern is the reason why Amos would kill his master, it gained him nothing. He was only employed by Mr Mason, he would not be able to rise up into another position within the company by killing Mr Mason, what could he hope to profit by it?"

John Mason squirmed a little in his seat but said nothing. Small beads of sweat were forming across his forehead and he pulled out a grubby handkerchief and mopped them away from his eyes.

"Now" said Quinn "if there was a Will somewhere that told us Amos was going to inherit the business then that would be a good motive but the only Will we have found gives you the business. So unless Amos thought he would gain something in your eyes by killing his Master, I am stuck to see his reasoning."

"I never gave Amos any idea I would grant him any favours. I've always said that my father was too soft on those three men. That they wouldn't last long if I was in control. Grubby, sneaking men those three monkeys are."

The Governor winced slightly and Quinn smiled.

"Of course, I totally understand, your father took those men on when you were still a boy, they've been around the whole time, insinuating themselves in your father's good books, not letting him see the worth of you, how you were his son, his natural heir. He sent you away, years spent overseas whilst those three villains worked on your father, stopped him thinking of making you the rightful owner of the business."

"That's right Detective Quinn, he sent me away, my own father and when I came back with plans for the business, we could have worked together and made the business really something, he said no. I had made contacts, real business contacts, we would have been stupendously rich but he always said no. They changed him, made him soft."

"Then Amos deserves to hang."

"They all deserve to hang, I hate them all, they sneer at me, talk about me in whispers, turn the men on the dock against me, so that I can't get things done, no-one respects me, they have done this to me, it's their fault and they must pay for it."

"And Amos is going to pay isn't he, with his life."

"Yes" said John and he shook with glee at the sight in his head.

"Except, we don't have any motive," said Quinn.

"What, why, what do, that shouldn't matter, you have him," words stumbled out of John's mouth, he looked furtively around the room.

"There's no reason for Amos to kill your father, he must know you hate him. With Mr Mason dead and his Will giving you the business, Amos and his friends will be out of job, penniless, destitute, they all have families, what will happen to them if they have no work."

"I don't care what happens to them, they have stolen my birthright."

"But they haven't, the Will gives you the business, you will inherit, Amos will hang and his family and his friends' families will all be ruined. So why would Amos kill Mr Mason, as long as he was alive he had a job, dead he has nothing."

John Mason blinked rapidly and his head twitched with annoyance. Polly could see him struggling not to blurt out that there was another Will.

"He must have had a reason, otherwise why did he kill my father, you should be questioning him, not me, find out what his reason was."

"Oh we have questioned him, Mr Mason," said the Governor, "he swears he's innocent. Not that I believe him of course as in the course of our, intense questioning he did admit that there was another Will, one that gave him and his partners the business and disowned yourself."

"I knew it, I knew that."

"Then why didn't you tell us Mr Mason, I assure you that the questioning that Amos went through was far more painful than this. He had a reason for not admitting there was a second Will, you should have put this information to us immediately, what did it behove you to keep this from us?" The Governor looked at him in interest; he was obviously beginning to understand what Quinn needed, thought Polly.

"Because the Will is nowhere to be found, I know the others searched for it and I did but I couldn't find it, my father had hidden it and it couldn't be found. It won't ever be found."

"A shame because without it Amos has no motive, it is rather you that has the motive," said Quinn.

"Perhaps we should conduct a full search of your father's property, both house and warehouse, to see if the Will has been hidden somewhere," said the Governor, "could you do that Detective Quinn?"

"I have already set that in motion Governor, my men were at both places at dawn this morning searching, if we are lucky the Will shall be found and this matter can be resolved."

"Perfect because I want to see the prisoner hanged for his crime but at the moment I would not be happy to do that, the situation is far more complicated than I was led to believe. There are questions I would have answered."

"But it won't be found," said John Mason, "it can't be found, it isn't there, it doesn't exist, you won't find it, I mean it won't be found, it…."

He carried on babbling as suddenly footsteps were heard running down the corridor and the door sprang open. Will entered and came to a sudden halt and held up a roll of paper tied up in red ribbon. Everyone turned to look at him in expectation.

"We found it Detective Quinn, the Will, we got it."

John Mason starred at him, he shook his head from side to side frantically and then he spoke.

"But you can't have found it I burnt it."

Silence fell as everyone turned to look at John Mason. He stared at them in horror.

"You burnt it?" asked Quinn quietly "where?"

John Mason's shoulders slumped in defeat.

"In my father's office."

"But you haven't been in your father's office for weeks according to what you have told us. I found warm ash in your father's grate, the morning his body was found, was it then you burnt it?"

"Yes" whispered John Mason.

The Governor leaned forward and stared at him.

Quinn went over to Will who passed him the ice pike, still wrapped in the handkerchief. Quinn went back to the table and placed it in front of John Mason. He looked at it and all the colour disappeared from his face.

"You recognise this don't you?" said Quinn, "we found it at the back of the warehouse; I'm guessing it is your father's blood on it and your fingerprints on the handle."

John Mason looked up at Quinn.

"We also found this," Quinn reached into his jacket pocket and took out a small dark lump of opium and placed it next to the ice pike. John Mason looked at and he licked his lips to bring moisture back to them, he groaned in desire and went to pick up the opium but Quinn was quicker.

"You need to tell us what happened before I give you this."

"I need that, you don't understand, it keeps me going, I need it."

"And you will get it, as soon as you tell us the truth."

John Mason reached out towards Quinn but then let his hands fall back into his lap and tears fell down his face.

"I just wanted him to see I could succeed. I was bringing in good money, I was going to be rich but then he threw it all back into my face. Told me he didn't approve of what I was doing, told me he had rewritten his Will. That the next morning he was going to disown me and the hated three would take over the business and I would be cast out. I had to stop him, don't you see, he was wrong, the business was mine. We argued and the next thing I knew I had picked up the ice pick and stabbed him. He looked at me, tried to say something and then fell down dead. I didn't know what to do, I panicked. I could hear people still moving around outside, so I just picked him up and hid him on top of the fish crate and went out for the evening. Telling everyone they could have an early night and we would carry on the next day. I wandered around not knowing what to do and then it hit me, a way to put the blame on to those I hated. I went back, picked up my father's body, carried him up to the house, used my key to let myself in, carried him into his office, pushed the letter opener into the hole where I had used the ice pick. I found the Will and burnt it in the grate and then left the way I had come and waited.

It was all going as I had hoped, Amos was arrested, his family were distraught, it was wonderful but then you came asking questions, I thought if I waited long enough you would leave everything alone and I would get away with it."

The Governor stood up and looked at Quinn.

"Well done Detective, you have proved me wrong and shown me that there is at least one man in this prison that is innocent. I will get my men to escort Mr Mason here to a more suitable room and ensure that Amos is freed immediately."

He bowed to Quinn and then to Polly before leaving the room without a further glance towards John Mason who sat crumpled in the chair.

No one said anything and it wasn't long before they heard the sound of the guards coming along the corridor. The same one they had met the previous day came in, chuckling to himself.

"You did it, didn't you, saved your man from the gallows but gave us one in return, thank you kindly for that I would 'ate to see the gallows deprived of its victim." He looked at the man that had come in with him and gestured to John Mason. "If you would be so kind."

The man went over to John Mason and fastened the leg and wrist irons on to him without problems then stood up and dragged John Mason up and then pushed him out of the door.

"If you three would follow me, I can escort you to the entrance where I assure you we will meet up with Mr Waters, now that he is a free man."

The guard turned and led them out of the dark prison and into the street outside, where indeed Amos was stood waiting for them, shaking a little in the cold morning air.

"You did it. Col told me to believe in you and you did it. How can I ever thank you?"

Polly walked over to him and hugged him.

"Keep the Mason Shipping Company going in the manner that Mr Mason would have wanted, have a good life that is all the thanks we need," Polly said as she let go and smiled at him.

"Amos" came a shout from behind them and they saw Col running towards them. He picked Amos up and swung him around in a joyous hug and put him down with a whoop of joy.

He turned to look at Polly and Will.

"Thank you my friends, you have proved yourself again, ask anything of me and I shall be yours to command," he turned to Quinn. "I'm sorry I don't know you."

"Let me introduce you to Detective Alec Quinn," said Polly and laughed when she saw Col's expression darken. "You must thank him as well Col, he believed in Amos and helped a lot in proving his innocence, without him we couldn't have done anything."

Col put out his hand; Quinn took it and shook it. "Then I must thank you with all my heart Detective Quinn. Strange as it is for me to offer my hand to a member of the law establishment, I trust that we will always be on the same side as it would seem a dangerous thing to have you on my tail. I hope that we may be friends instead."

"Nor would I like the task of taking you into jail, so stay out of trouble my friend."

"I will do my best Sir. Now there is a very reputable restaurant around the corner that I have encouraged to open for us this morning, your family is there Amos, as are George and Henry with their families. They are waiting to celebrate your release. What do you say to joining them and raising a glass to the future?"

"Col you are a true friend, lead on, I am famished and yearn to see my family," said Amos.

"The invitation is open to all of you," Col added as he saw Quinn began to turn away. Quinn stopped and looked at Col.

"Thank you kindly. I will gladly take you up on that offer," said Quinn, "it is not often that I get to celebrate happy endings."

Polly took Col's hand. "Lead on Col, we are with you, let us enjoy our victory."

Col led them along the street and they left the darkness of the jail and all thoughts of the fate of John Mason behind them.

THE CASE OF THE WOLFPACK KILLERS

1 THE BODY

Polly woke as she heard Will go past her door and the stairs creak and groan as he made his way down them. Opening her eyes she tried to see the clock on her bedside table, but her bedroom was too dark. Through a gap in her curtains, the gas lamps in the street outside sent a flickering light across her bed but there was no other light to help her see anything. Obviously dawn was still a long way off. Who on earth would be knocking on the shop front door in the middle of the night, she wondered.

Whatever was going on she didn't want to know. The air in her bedroom was cold but she was nice and warm under the heavy eiderdown on her bed. She snuggled back down and pulled the bedding up to her chin and shut her eyes. She hoped that Will would be able to deal with whatever had woken him and sent him downstairs to investigate. Maybe it was just a vagrant who had disturbed him whilst making a bed for themselves in the shop doorway or some revellers making too much noise as they staggered home.

Her hopes were destroyed though when she heard his footsteps come back upstairs and stop outside her door and softly knock. She sat up in bed and called out for him to come in. The door opened and an arm holding a candle appeared, closely followed by the rest of Will looking apologetic.

"There's a young peeler downstairs, says he's been sent by Quinn to get us. Seems there's a body he wants us to look at. He doesn't want anyone else but us sent for, the young lad seems most put out that he's 'ad to come and fetch us, don't think he approves of the likes of us."

Polly yawned and threw back the eiderdown and got out of bed, shivering a little as the cold air hit her skin.

"I doubt Quinn would have informed him of why he wanted us, so the young man probably doesn't see why Quinn would need a detective agency to come and help when he has the whole of the London police force at his back. Let's not keep him waiting, lest he feels his job is done and he disappears on us."

"I'll get ready quickly then and hurry down 'nd keep him company until you're ready."

He disappeared and shut the door behind him and Polly struck a match to light the candle she kept by her bed.

After a quick wash in the cold water from the basin sat on her chest of drawers she pulled on trousers and a shirt and leather waistcoat. If she was being pulled out of her comfy, warm bed in the early hours of the morning she was dammed if she was going to bother to dress up for the occasion. She pulled her hair up and twined it into as neat a bun as she could, pinning it into place and ignoring the strands that swung free to fall around her face. Pulling on long socks and then knee-high boots which she laced up tightly, she began to feel ready for Quinn and whatever grisly business he wanted to present to her and Will.

Taking her long black coat from the hook behind her door and swinging herself into it, she made her way downstairs where she found Will and Gadget waiting for her. Will looked at her and saw her glance towards Gadget and shrugged.

"She heard me talking to you and by the time I got down here she was waiting for us. Says she wants to come too and nothing we say will put her off."

"That's what I said and I mean it, I'm coming with you, whatever you say," said Gadget "if'n you leave me behind I'll follow you so don't bother to try and leave me 'ere."

"Did I say anything" said Polly.

"No, just making meself clear on the subject."

"Very well, but please just stay back a bit when we get there. I doubt Quinn would be happy to see one as young as you at a crime scene."

"He don't know much about me then does he?"

"No he doesn't Gadget but humour me please."

"Alright, I'll 'ang back, unless there's something that I think I can do."

Will looked out of the shop window and turned back to Polly.

"The lad's got a cab outside Polly, I don't think he wants to 'ang around for much longer, I reckon we should get going," he said.

"Well, I trust he sent a cab that can fit us all. Let's go and see what Quinn needs us for, shall we?"

They left the building, Polly ensuring that the door was locked securely behind them and climbed up into the cab. The young lad looked askance at

Gadget clambering in encumbered, as always, with her oversized leather shoulder bag. She just stared at him in defiance and he looked away, tapped on the ceiling of the cab and called out to the cabbie.

"Back to Detective Quinn please."

The driver clicked his whip and the horses pulled the cab away.

They travelled along in silence for a while and Polly could feel sleep trying to claim her as the sounds of the horses' hooves and the wheels of the cab rocking over the cobbles began to relax her. She shook herself, pulled herself a little more upright and looked across at the young lad who had been sent to summon them. He looked only a little older than Gadget with the very faint beginnings of a beard and a shock of dark brown hair that looked as though he would always fail to keep it neat. Polly surmised that either he was always unkempt or he had dressed quickly as one of the buttons on his jacket was undone and a small bit of white showed where he hadn't quite managed to fully tuck his shirt into his trousers. He was still sending sideway glances towards Gadget; obviously not at all sure she should be there. Gadget kept grinning at him, enjoying his discomfiture and not helping him to relax in the slightest.

"Do you know why Quinn needs us?" asked Polly, in the hope that she could help the young lad to relax a little.

The boy brought his attention away from Gadget and he looked across at Polly.

"Sorry Miss, I don't. He just called me over and told me where you lived and to go and knock on the door until someone answered and then to get you to 'im."

"I take it a crime has been discovered, Will said you told him something about a body?"

"Yes Miss, there's a body down by the river, don't know why Quinn wants you though. If you ask me it's just another drunk that fell in the Thames."

"Well, I'm afraid, that if Quinn is asking for us I have a feeling your idea might not be correct."

The boy shrugged as though what he believed was far more likely than what Quinn had said and Polly decided not to pursue the topic further. She relaxed back into the cab's leather seating, if that was all the information the young man had on the subject there was nothing more to do but wait whilst the cab took them to Quinn. It rattled along the cobbled streets dipping in and out of shadows as they passed lit streets and dark alleyways. Occasionally they caught the sound of the night inhabitants, women in the dark, braving the cold night air, looking for another client. Some of them had shawls and gloves on, other were in little more than a petticoat and simple bodice, all trying to entice someone to spend a bit of time with them. They passed men staggering home their bellies full of bad ale and their voices sounding loud in the night airs as they regaled their companions with stories about their evening's entertainment. Cabs went past them, their cabbies flicking their whips and the horses' hooves clattering on the cobbles.

Finally the cab came to a halt along the embankment of the Thames. The young man got out and held the door open for the three to disembark. He pointed to steps leading down to the river bank, Polly could hear the murmur of voices and the sharp tone of Quinn ordering men to keep clear and just wait.

"We'd better get down there, seems we have kept them all waiting," said Polly and hurried over to the steps and made her way down. Quinn looked up as he caught sight of them and visibly sighed in relief. He gestured quickly for them to make their way over to him.

At the bottom of the steps wide planks of wood had been laid out providing a pathway to where a dark shape showed where the body lay crumpled on the wet mud. Lights on stands precariously balanced on wooden squares helped to illuminate the sad sight. Quinn was anxiously looking towards the water's edge aware that the tide would soon be coming in and then the body would have to be moved and any evidence would be lost.

Polly led the way over to him and he smiled as she came close.

"Thank you for coming, there isn't much time left before the tide turns but I wanted you two to see him whilst the victim was here, rather than back in the morgue. I always think looking at a body where it is found will tell any investigator worth their salt more than can be seen when it has been taken away."

"How can we help?"

"You know how I like to work. Please just have a look and tell me what strikes you."

"Three things off, are they Quinn?" asked Will.

"Just give me what you think and then I'll tell you what I think."

Will nodded and stepped forward crouching down by the body and sniffing. He looked up at the high stone wall in front of him and then behind him at the river.

"Are we alright to touch or move him Quinn?" asked Polly.

"Yes, I've got all the notes I need and photos have been taken."

Polly crouched down next to Will and leant over the body. It was a middle-aged man, certainly not a rich man; his clothes were old and serviceable, though now they showed signs of being scuffed and torn. Polly picked out a holly leaf from one tear along the arm of his jacket.

"We found a few of those on him, seems he must have tried to get through a holly bush or fallen into one not long before he died," said Quinn.

Polly picked up the man's right hand and saw that the knuckles were bruised and torn. She gently placed it back down on the ground and looked at his face. That too showed signs of a fight, a bruise had begun to form above his right eye and a trickle of blood had seeped out of a cut on his jaw. She opened up his shirt and inspected his torso, deep bruising and more scratches showed across his midriff.

"Are you getting anything Pol?" asked Will.

"He's been dead too long Will, any echoes of his death that might have been there are long gone, all we have is what our eyes and your nose can tell us."

"Have a look at the bottom of his trousers, that ain't Thames mud on 'em."

Polly moved round Will to crouch at the man's feet.

"You're right, the Thames mud is brown, and the mud on his trousers is redder in colour. Do you need any more time?"

She looked across at Will.

"No I've seen enough", he said. Polly stood up and looked at Quinn.

"We've got what we need, what happens now?"

"Now I have to get that body back to the morgue, then wait on the photographer to give me some copies of the man's face, which will take too long, then I have to find out who he is and work from there."

"I can get you copies quicker," said Gadget.

Quinn jumped as she spoke and he turned and tried to see who had spoken. Gadget was stood just outside the line of light, so he had missed seeing her arrive. She smiled at him then looked at Polly.

"I stayed out the way Polly, like I promised but I can help now," she said.

"Is this child with you?" said Quinn obviously not happy about her being there.

"Quinn meet Gadget, Gadget this is Detective Quinn."

"You brought a child to a crime scene."

"Not exactly," said Polly

"I'm a part of Baker & Dagger Investigators, I am Mr Quinn, so don't you say I'm just a child. I may well be that but I grew up on the streets and I'm older than I look. But that don't matter now, cause I can 'elp you. Cause I can get a likeness of that man out on the streets quicker than your photographer can and I'm not scared to look at a dead man."

Polly sighed. "You may as well let her come in closer Quinn; she is not easy to say no to."

"If you believe it will be okay then I bow to your judgement Polly."

Quinn shrugged and gestured Gadget to come forward.

She walked up to the man, crouched down and taking a sketch pad and pencil from her bag proceed to sketch his likeness.

Polly and Will stepped closer to Quinn and let Gadget have as much light as possible to continue drawing.

Quinn looked back at Gadget, shrugged as he saw the determination in her young face as she started to draw. He looked back at Polly and Will.

"What did you find; do you have an idea of what happened to this unfortunate man?"

"What we believe happened Quinn, is that he did not die here. He was in a fight with possibly multiple opponents and somewhere along the line tried to escape through holly and sharp-thorned bushes. That's our conclusion isn't it Will, have I missed anything?"

"I reckon he was dumped 'ere from up top, sometime earlier this evening, rather than brought 'ere by boat," added Will.

"Do you mind telling me what brings you both to those conclusions?" asked Quinn.

"The tears in his clothing, some obviously made by him being pushed into a holly tree or running into one, but there are others more ragged, indicating different foliage. His injuries, well I've seen Will battered and bruised before now and know that different people punch in different ways and with differing power. There were a few harder punches laid on that man and a few lighter ones, ergo more than one opponent. It also looks like he has been kicked; I would hazard a guess that some of his ribs are broken."

"And the time he got here and your belief that he was dumped from the road side rather than pushed over the side of a boat?" asked Quinn.

"If he had been pushed into the river at high tide and his body carried to this place, his clothes would be sodden and the red mud on his trousers would have been washed away. Will's right, if we look at the alternative. It would make sense with his condition that he was thrown over the side of the wall above us sometime after high tide as the mud hasn't yet seeped fully into his clothing. Whoever left him here was either totally confident that nothing would lead back to them or incredibly arrogant. Looking at all the information we have already deciphered I would chose the latter. Whoever it was you can be sure you have our complete assistance in finding them."

"But you already knew all this didn't you Quinn? What made you send for us?" asked Will.

Quinn pushed his hands into his pockets and sighed.

"He's not the first I've found in this state, but I want him to be the last. All I have is a series of bodies that show signs of rough treatment, in torn clothing with traces of red mud on them. Nothing to tell me who they were or where they were when they died. My other problem is no one will talk to me, I'm the law and as such not to be trusted. I have run into dead ends across the breadth of the city."

"Difficult indeed, the idea of a police force is still new to a lot of people and trust is hard to gain in this city," said Polly.

"Finished," said Gadget and she came over to them holding the sketch pad for their viewing.

Quinn looked at it and smiled.

"It's a good likeness of him, you've taken out the bruising and cuts on his face," he said.

"Made sense to, people will know him as he was, not all battered and bashed like he is now. I will get you multiple copies by lunchtime."

Quinn smiled again, "You're pretty sure of yourself, young lady, how are you going to do that?"

"I have a gadget that will sort it out, don't you worry Mr Detective."

"Really, well I shall look forward to seeing the results."

The young man who had brought them came forward.

"The cart is here Detective Quinn, for the body."

"Thank you, go and tell the men to bring it over. There is nothing more we can do here. Thank you Polly, Will and Gadget. I'll arrange for you to get home and see you later with the copies. Thank you for your insight."

"I don't think we told you anything more than you already knew," said Polly.

"You confirmed that which I already knew yes but I am hoping that you will consider following your own lines of enquiry. You can go to places that I cannot and there are skills that you have which I cannot aspire to. If I learn anything more from the body I will let you know."

"We will do what we can Quinn, I promise. Now we had better get home and get some sleep, there are still a few hours left before dawn."

Quinn smiled at them and called the young policeman over. Two men came across the wooden planks pulling a simple two wheeled cart and proceeded to pick up the body and place it on the cart. Quinn turned to the young policeman.

"Hail a cab and give him instructions to take these three home again."

The young man gave a nod and ran back to the steps and up and out of sight.

By the time Polly, Will and Gadget had made it to the street there was a cab waiting for them. They gratefully got in and let the horse and cabbie take them home.

2 CLUES

It was early the next morning, after struggling to get back to sleep following their disturbed night that Polly got up and decided that she may as well see what Gadget had planned for replicating the drawing she had made of the dead man.

She walked into Gadget's workshop, which had started out as a wood store in the back yard behind the shop but after numerous entreaties by Gadget, Mr Hardaker had relented and agreed to change it. He and Will, under the watchful eye of Gadget, had created a workspace which fulfilled her every need. Shelves lined one wall, on which she had placed wooden boxes which were full of bits and pieces of old metal toys, clocks, cogs and wheels and anything that Gadget found that she thought would come in useful at some point. They had also rigged up a work table with a sheet of wood on top hinged so that it could be raised up on an angle for her to use as a drawing easel. On to this board Gadget had rigged up a system so that through a system of pencils, cogs, string and slim lengths of wood all connected together and held between two runners top and bottom of it she could copy from one picture onto six other pieces of paper. Polly watched as she traced over the drawing of the dead man and his likeness appeared on six pieces of paper attached to the board.

"I've already got eighteen done, with this six there will be twenty-four, do you reckon that would be enough?" Gadget asked without looking up from her work.

"Plenty I should think. Did you get any sleep?"

"A little bit but I was itching to get this done so as soon as I had light enough I came out and got started. There, finished," she said and yawned. Carefully taking out the six copies she handed them to Polly and yawned again.

"Perhaps you should go and get some sleep now. Will and I can take this out and get the search started for who this man is."

Gadget looked at her and scowled.

"No, I want to go and give these to the Detective, show him that I can do it, I don't think he believed me," she said.

"Well, let's go in and see if Will is up, if so you and he can go and see Quinn. I have someone else I want to take some copies to."

"That wouldn't be someone who has Col as his friend would it?" said Will from the doorway.

Polly turned round and smiled. "He is the other side of the law, a person that Quinn can't get to but I can. Let's see if I am as safe walking through Soho as Col claimed I would be after helping Amos."

"Just make sure you 'ave something up your sleeve in case you aren't."

"Don't worry about me I'll be fine."

"I know you will, I just like to worry a bit about you sometimes, makes me feel better."

"You will have your hands full looking after Gadget. I doubt the incumbents of the police station will ever have met someone like her."

"'Ere what do you fink I'm going to do there, Polly, I can behave when I want to and I want Quinn to be impressed with what I've done. I'm not stupid. If I behave when I go today, he might listen to me in the future, especially if I deliver what I promised to him last night."

"Very well, we shall share a cab as far as Soho and then you can go on to visit Quinn, whilst I enter into Innocent's domain."

Polly got down from the cab as they got to the outskirts of Soho and waved the cabbie on to continue taking Will and Gadget to see Quinn. She stepped from the broad thoroughfare into the dark small street and the sunshine seemed to dim a little as she did so. The tall thin buildings seemed to loom over the narrow roads. Pale faces looked out of dirty windows at her but no one ventured out to accost her. She passed a woman sitting on a doorstep, her makeup looking gaudy and over done in the morning light, her dress was tattered and the ribbons on her dress were so dirty Polly was hard pressed to work out what their original colour might have been. She sneered and went to say something but then focused on Polly's face and instead attempted a smile. Which, Polly thought to herself, might have worked better if she had all her teeth. Instead her grin showed a mouth with gaps and brown pegs that were all that were left to chew her food with.

"Morning Miss Baker, I 'ope all is well with you."

"Thank you, it is," Polly said. "I'm sorry but how do you know who I am?"

"We all know who you are Miss Baker; we know what you did for Col's friend and Mr Innocent. Everyone in this part of London knows who you are; you're one of the good 'uns."

"That's very kind of you, I only did what I felt was the right thing to do. Amos was innocent of any crime. I hope that you won't think me rude but I need to see Mr Innocent, I beg your leave." She smiled at the lady hoping that her horror at the woman's appearance was not apparent on her face.

"He'll be glad to see you Miss, you's a favourite of 'is. He's told everyone that you's his special girl. You 'urry along there, don't mind about me."

Polly smiled and walked swiftly away, though she was certainly going to have a strong word with Innocent when she found him. After a few more people had stopped to doff their caps to her and one woman had actually curtsied Polly began to realise just how much influence Innocent and Col had over Soho, "It might make it easier for me to walk through here, but the fact that the whole of Soho thinks I'm Innocent's special girl is rather insulting," she thought to herself.

It only took her a short while to get to the small square that was home of The Hangman's Dance and as she looked up at the swinging sign she heard Col's voice calling to her from the top of the stone steps to the side of the building.

"Good morning Polly, how nice to see you, to what do we owe this visit?"

"Good morning Col, I need to speak to you and Innocent, I have a picture of a man I need you to look at."

"Innocent has just got up, so you are in good time. Come on down and I may even be able to offer you some breakfast if you wished it."

"I would not say no to a cup of your coffee Col."

Col laughed and turned to go down the steps. Polly followed him and entered into Innocent's office. Innocent was sitting at his desk, a plate of food in front of him and a glass of wine to one side. His dark hair was tousled, half pulled back into a leather band with strands escaping to frame his face, which showed dark stubble along his jaw line. His shirt was undone and looked as though it had just been thrown on when he had risen from his bed. All in all she admitted to herself he looked a very pretty package, it was a shame that he was on the other side of the legal code that she herself believed in.

He looked up as she entered and a smile tugged at the edge of his lips. "To what do we owe this pleasure, Miss Baker? I did not think you would frequent this part of town, especially not at this hour of the day. I trust you had no problem getting to me."

"No problem at all thank you, though I dread to think what you have told everyone, they seem to think I am more to you than I actually am."

"Perhaps."

Polly looked at him but Innocent didn't add any further comment.

"You said you wanted us to look at a picture," Col said to break the silence.

"You haven't lost someone have you, is there a rival to my affection?" said Innocent as he raised an eyebrow and smiled at her.

"No, this man is dead and Detective Quinn wants to find out who he is and why he died."

Innocent looked aghast as her, "Detective Quinn? You consort with the law; how dare you step into my office and mention such a person."

"I mention him because he cannot enter this establishment and he needs your help. You would do well to treat him as well as you treat me."

"I can hardly hold him in my affections as sweetly as I hold you, Polly my dear."

"Will you be serious, Innocent. Quinn is a good man and you would do well to get on his good side, he cares about his job and what he stands for."

Innocent looked at her, leaned back in his chair and then smiled.

"I am sorry, Polly, you find me in a combative mood this morning, I think the wind is changing direction. Please sit down, I apologise for my appearance but it was a late night. Col please get Polly a seat and a drink. Then when we have passed the time of day a little you can show me the picture and I will tell you if I recognise the man."

Polly went to get the drawings from her bag, but Innocent raised a hand.

"Please, sit, I do not wish to see the face of a dead man before I have finished my coffee. The man is dead, I'm sure he will not be any deader if you have a cup with me."

Polly sighed and sat down in the chair Col brought over to the desk. Col brought one over for himself and then went to get another cup and poured out a coffee for her from a tall silver pot that was stood on the desk.

"Would you like some sugar or cream Polly?" he asked.

"Just some cream please Col."

Col delicately poured the cream so that it sat on the top of the rich dark brew and passed the dainty cup across to Polly. She took a sip and sighed, it was far better than any blend that she was able to afford. She thought to herself that she could happily get used to such coffee each morning. Then she pulled herself up short as she thought on how insidious the lifestyle of Innocent and Col was to the unwary. Was enjoying the coffee the first step over which she would trip and find herself being drawn in to accepting the way in which it had provided Innocent with the funds to buy it.

"It is just a cup of coffee, Polly, which I promise was fairly bought."

Polly smiled, could the man read her mind she wondered. She looked at him and saw something in his eyes, maybe Innocent wasn't as easy to understand as she had previously thought. There was a hurt in his eyes which belied the easy words he spoke. She put down the cup.

"It is lovely, thank you Innocent," she said, "may I show you the drawing now."

"Please," he said leaning forward to put his elbows on the desk, "let us see this corpse. Though I don't know why you think I would know him. Not every murder victim will have passed through Soho; this is not the crime centre of the city."

"I did not think that they would have. Quinn wanted us to get the drawing to as many as people as we could and understands that you can get it to more people than he can. I have some copies of it, if you want to distribute them around to people." She picked the drawings that Gadget had done out of her bag and passed them over to Innocent. He took them and looked at them for a moment before handing one to Col with a sigh.

"I don't think we need to have any copies, I know who that is, don't you Col?"

Col looked at the drawing and frowned, "Yes, that's Ralph, Betsy's man. He never did anyone any harm, what happened to him Polly?"

"That's what Quinn wants to find out, his body was found on the bank of the Thames, he'd been beaten up and killed. Quinn says he wasn't the first but he hasn't been able to find any leads as to who is killing people."

"Are you saying there are more people like him, beaten up and killed, and we don't know about it?"

"Will and I have just been called on board, Innocent. Quinn has tried to find out who the other victims are but has not met with any success. It seems the disreputable side of society does not wish to help him."

"Perhaps that can change. For now Col, go and see if you can find Betsy. Tell her to come and see us, let's see if she can shine any light onto what Ralph had got himself into."

Col nodded and left, in a few seconds they saw him run up the steps and disappear from view.

"Come, sit by the fire and tell me more about this Detective Quinn and how you found Ralph."

Polly went over to one of the chairs and sat down, Innocent sat down opposite her.

"Quinn sent for us last night and we were taken to where Ralph's body had been found, he'd been dumped on the banks of the Thames. It was obvious that he had not died there, his clothes were torn and a few holly leaves were found caught in the cloth. His face was bruised and battered, his knuckles too."

"So he fought then, hopefully he took someone out on his way down."

"I don't know, Innocent, there was no blood on him, it wasn't clear what had caused his death but from the look on his face he died scared."

"And no clue as to where he had been killed, other than holly leaves?"

"Red mud had covered his boots and trousers but that was it, nothing else, no easy piece of paper, saying please come here for your death, signed your helpful murderer."

"So your only clues are red mud and a holly leaf. You are looking for somewhere that has both, I wonder where..." he said and then he stopped and Polly could see something had occurred to him.

"Do those things mean something to you, Innocent?"

"I don't know, something tripped in my head, but I can't get the context. Never mind it will come to me, if I don't force it."

"Will you help us find out what happened? Will you tell Quinn if you know anything?"

"He was one of mine Polly; I will do all I can to help you find his killer, never fear. It is good that your detective wants to find out, I approve of a man who is concerned for the lower classes. It is nice to know, there are such men out there."

"He's a good man Innocent; I think you would like him."

"He's the law Polly, I doubt it, they don't tend to have much time for such as I." There was something behind his words that made Polly want to reach over and touch him but before she could act on her thought footsteps sounded on the steps and Innocent jumped out of the chair and went over to the door. He opened it to let Col come in with a young woman who looked as though she had just woken up. Though if she had, she had slept in the clothes she was wearing, Polly thought. She looked nervous about being in the company of Innocent and bobbed him a curtsey before standing there, her hands clasped together to stop them shaking.

Innocent gently took her arm and led her over to the chair he had just vacated.

"I'm sorry to disturb you Betsy and be assured you have done no wrong. I don't want to distress you but I need you to look at a drawing and tell me if you know who it is."

He handed her the piece of paper and she took it and gasped. "That's my Ralphie, why have you got a picture of 'im, what's going on?"

"Oh Betsy, I'm sorry, but Ralph is dead, he died yesterday and the peelers found his body by the Thames. I promise you that we are going to find out what happened to him and catch his killers. They will pay for what they did to him; you have my word on that."

"Ralphie's dead, but that can't be, nobody 'ad no reason to kill Ralphie, 'e was a good man, 'e never did nobody no 'arm, who'd want to kill 'im?" She burst into tears and Innocent pulled out a crisp white handkerchief from his trouser pocket. He handed it to her as he sat on the arm of the chair and put his arm around her, holding on to her as she cried. As her tears subsided, he let go and sank down to the floor to look up at her and get her attention.

"Betsy, I am going to find out what happened to him I promise and Miss Polly and a detective are going to help. But we need you to help us as well, can you think of anything that Ralph said to you recently that might give us a clue of where to start looking for his killers?"

Betsy started to shake her head but stopped and looked at Innocent.

"Oh it can't 'ave been, but it must 'ave been them."

"Who Betsy, who did Ralph speak about?" said Innocent.

"He said it was alright, that they was toffs, that it would be easy, 'e reckoned we were going to get away, get that place in the country he'd always dreamed of. I knew it sounded off like, but I couldn't get 'im to see it, I said toffs ain't any better'n the rest of us, they just do it with more money, but 'e couldn't see it."

"See what Betsy?"

She went to start crying again but Innocent gently touched her arm and she held back the sob. She looked at him with such a look of despair that Polly was tempted to send a calming spell towards her but then Betsy nodded.

"If'n I tell you all what I know, you'll catch 'em won't you Mr Innocent, you'll kill 'em won't you, 'e was a good man, 'e didn't deserve to die."

"I'll catch them, I promise but I need your help, please tell me what Ralph was getting into."

"He came to me a few weeks back, scared like, said someone was following 'im, said 'e couldn't work out who it was but they was there, just at the corner of his eye like. I reckoned 'e was seeing things, I mean who would be interested in someone like Ralph, so I told 'im not to worry his head about it all. Then a few days back 'e come bouncing in to me and says, 'e was right, they was following 'im but because 'e saw 'em they reckoned 'e was just the man they needed. So they was going to give 'im a job. I asked what job but 'e said 'e didn't know, 'e just had to go out to this big 'ouse and all would be explained. I didn't like the sound of it Mr Innocent I can tell you and I told Ralph so but he was so full of it, said they said 'e was important and would be one of a line of important people to them. He said 'e 'ad met the main man and he thought 'im ever so posh so 'e was going to do it."

"Did he say there was anything about this man that would give us a clue as to who he was? Anything Betsy, it could be something so small and insignificant but it might help?"

"There was something Mr Innocent but I don't know how it would 'elp, I mean you can't go up to all the toffs and ask can you?"

"Ask what Betsy?"

"To look at their right hand Mr Innocent, cause Ralph said that this man 'e only had three fingers, seemed 'e'd lost 'is little finger somehow. There was a right rough scar there, Ralph said."

Innocent looked at Betsy intently.

"He was missing his right little finger, that's what Ralph said, you're certain Betsy. The toff didn't have a little finger on his right hand?"

"That's what Ralph said Mr Innocent, is it important, can it 'elp catch 'im."

"Do you know who it is Innocent, does Ralph's description strike a chord?" asked Polly.

Innocent looked over at Col and then back to Polly. He looked as though he was about to say something but then shook his head.

"No, no I don't think so, it might be something but I don't know, nothing worth repeating at this moment in any case," he turned to Betsy "thank you, my dear, I am sorry about Ralph, you go on home now and take some rest, I will send Col with you and he will tell everyone what has happened and that you are allowed time to grieve, don't worry" he added as he saw concern on Betsy's face "I will ensure that you do not lose financially by not working for a while. Go home, rest and when you want to get back to work, you send me word."

He stood up, helped Betsy to her feet and led her over to Col who took her arm and went to lead her out. Betsy though turned and went to hand Innocent's handkerchief back.

"You keep that, I have more. I will find out what happened Betsy I promise."

She smiled at him and left with Col close behind her.

Innocent went over to the door and held it open.

"Thank you Polly for bringing the picture to us, I need to get on with some work so I will let you know if we find out any more," he said.

"You know who it is, don't you Innocent. You are going to track him down, please tell me you are going to be careful, he has killed more than one person. What are you going to do Innocent?"

"At this moment in time, nothing, I have a business to run, there is work to do. I will send word out that I want to know if any of my employees have seen or can be on the look out to see if they can find a man missing the little finger on his right hand. But until I hear back from them there is nothing I can do."

Polly looked up at him.

"I believe that you already know who he is. Will you promise me something? Don't go after him yourself Innocent; we can all go after him, backed by the full weight of the law."

Innocent looked at her in amazement and then laughed, took hold of her arm and led her towards the door.

"Trust me Polly, I have no intention of putting myself in danger but the idea of me being backed by the law is ludicrous. Now please, go back to your office, stay safe and I will let you know if I find out anything more."

With that he kissed her gently and pushed her out of the door, shutting it firmly in her face.

Polly stared at it for a few moments toying with the idea of blasting it back open but shrugged, what would be gained by showing Innocent that he had annoyed her. "He would probably think it meant I was attracted to him", she thought to herself and so instead left via the steps and made her way out of Soho, where she caught a cab and went back to the office.

3 ANOTHER EARLY MORNING

A furious knocking startled Polly from her sleep. As she opened her eyes to darkness she realised she was once again being woken up in the middle of the night.

"What now," she exclaimed "are we never to have a full night's sleep."

She climbed out of bed, grabbed her dressing gown, threw it around herself and was outside her bedroom door as Will came along the corridor.

"This is becoming a little too regular for my liking," he said as he passed her and ran down the stairs.

The door flew open as Will unlocked it and Col burst into the dark shop. The street light outside illuminated him enough for them to realise that something was very wrong. It was obvious that he had got dressed without thinking and at top speed. His clothes were in disarray, his shirt was hanging outside of his trousers and his waistcoat was unbuttoned and he was carrying a heavy overcoat.

"Col, what on earth is the matter," Polly asked.

"It's Innocent, he didn't come back."

"Back from where? What was he doing?" asked Will.

"I knew he knew something about Ralph's killer, he should have confided in me. Why didn't he ask for my help? Men! Sometimes they need their heads examined," said Polly.

"We've got to find him, Polly; I can feel that something is terribly wrong. Please help me." Col grabbed hold of Polly's hands and she could feel him shaking with fear.

"Of course, we'll help. Col wait here, Will and I will get dressed and be with you in moments."

"What's going on, what's all the racket?" asked Gadget from the top of the stairs.

"Perfect timing Gadget, I have a task for you. Get dressed; we have an emergency on our hands. I need you to find Detective Quinn for us."

Gadget spun on her heels and disappeared from view.

"Polly we can't wait for the law to help us. Please Polly, there is no time to lose; by the time they get here it might be too late."

"Col, nothing will be gained by us running off all on our own with no backup to follow. Trust us, and in this case, Quinn. He will come to our aid, I know he will. He is just as invested in finding these killers and deserves to be included in any action that we take on. Will and I will come with you now but I want the assistance the law can give us afterwards. I will send Gadget to go and find Quinn; we can always leave him messages, if we find any clues. Now give me leave to get dressed, I am not chasing after Innocent in my nightgown."

Col nodded at her and she gave him a quick hug before turning and running back up to her bedroom. She got dressed as quickly as she could, but even so Will and Gadget were running down the stairs before her. Gadget was inevitably carrying her large bulky bag.

"We need you to move fast young lady, do you have to take that with you," said Polly.

"You never know what we are going to 'ave to do Polly, I can perform wonders with what I carry in this."

"Very well, I will not question you, I do not have time and you've proved your worth too many times before. Now I need you to go back to where you went with Will to see Detective Quinn, hopefully he will still be there, knowing him he will be. You must convince him that we need his help. Tell him that Innocent has worked out who the killer of Ralph might be and went by himself to try and find him. He has subsequently disappeared. Col, Will and I are going to see if we can find him, we will leave messages or signs on our route to show you where we have gone, but get Quinn, by whatever means you can. We will need the law at the end of this night I am sure of it." She gave Gadget some money "There is enough there for a cab fare, we need you to move fast."

"It's all very well me giving him the message but where do I take him to pick up the trail? Col, do you know where Innocent went this evening?" asked Gadget.

"He went to the old Gentlemen's Club at the edge of the city; I don't know if you've ever been there. It's known as The Last Stand, cause it's really selective about its membership."

"I know it," said Gadget. "I dipped a few pockets from the rich buggers who went there. Afore I was part of Baker and Dagger, Polly, 'onest, I ain't done any of that recently, cross me heart and 'ope to die, promise."

Polly sighed.

"Go and get Quinn, we will talk about your language and previous behaviour later."

Gadget disappeared out of the door and her fast footsteps rang out on the cobbles.

"Right Col, we'll go to the club."

"Thank you Polly, I've got a cab waiting for us."

"Let's get going then before we wake up all the neighbours," said Will.

They went out into the street and Will turned and locked the shop door behind them. The cab was waiting right by the kerb with a very nervous cabbie sitting in the driving seat.

"Take us to The Last Stand and then you get on home," said Col as he helped Polly into the cab.

"Yes Sir, Mr Colossus, Sir," the man stammered and set his horses moving at a fast pace as soon as Col shut the cab door.

"He seems a little anxious, do you have that effect on everyone you deal with?" asked Polly as she grabbed at the side of the cab as it careered around a corner.

"I didn't have time to be polite, I will apologise to him tomorrow," growled Col.

The cab rattled along for a few minutes and then slammed to a halt throwing Polly into Will. Col opened the door and was out and heading towards the large dark building in front of them before either of them could get themselves separated and out of the cab.

"At this rate we'll be dead before we ever get a chance to find Innocent," grumbled Will as he clambered out of the cab and helped Polly down.

"He's worried about his friend, be patient with him."

Humph was the only reply she got as Will followed after Col.

"It looks shut up for the night, let's not go banging on any more doors please Col," said Polly as she saw Col raise a fist to start knocking, "Where do all the horses get stabled whilst their owners are indulging themselves, we may pick up some clues there," she continued.

Col looked at her, then lowered his arm and led them both around the left-hand side of the building to where a large gate stood closed.

"Do you want me to break in?" he asked.

"Only if we really need to, hopefully we can pick something up out here. I would rather guess that Innocent is not inside. If something has happened to him, he is either already dead or has been taken somewhere, either way we should be able to pick up some hint of him from here. Can you find any trace of him Will?"

"I 'ave Innocent's smell in my 'ead from our time in 'is safe house and from your clothes after you've visited 'im Polly, so I'll give it go."

He went up to the gate and began to walk along the wall beside it and then went back over the same patch of ground again. He stopped, knelt down and sniffed the ground.

"Got him, but there's something else 'ere. There's the faint smell of Innocent but overlying that a stronger scent, it's why I missed it the first time round. I can smell chloroform and something else Polly, I know the scent but can't grab 'old of the memory."

"Follow the chloroform then Will, see where it leads. I think Innocent found the killer but got caught out. If they drugged him, he's still alive. Come on Col, the hunt is afoot now, we have a chance. They won't be expecting anyone to have worked out that Innocent is missing, so may make some mistakes. We must keep faith that there is enough time for us to catch up with them."

Will set off along the road and at each turn or junction in the road he hesitated a moment before leading them on. Polly marked on a wall or signpost in chalk at each change in direction.

"Can't we go any faster?" said Col.

"Where to, Col? Will's the best there is at this, trust him, he will find Innocent. If he's survived this long we have to trust he will survive for a bit longer and we have to leave a clear trail for Quinn and Gadget."

Will suddenly stopped at a junction where the road in one direction lead back into town and the other led out in the countryside that surrounded London. He turned to look at Polly.

"I can still smell the trail but I am pretty certain that I know where we need to go. If I'm right, I don't need to follow the trail anymore and we can move a lot faster. Do you remember this road Polly? We used to go this way a lot when we was kids."

Polly looked at him curiously then at the road they had joined. She looked around herself and then realised what Will had meant.

"Of course, the old Brigadier, his house is out that way, the maze in his grounds, holly, thorns, red mud, oh we have been dim."

"It's been over ten years and we was just children then, why should we 'ave remembered."

"But the cruelty of it all should have triggered something in us. I would wager that a certain person has gone from bullying small children to murder. We'll need faster transport now Col, we know where we are going and who we are up against. Do you have any connections around here that could supply us with transportation?"

"There's a stable over that way, just a few yards down the road. Innocent and I have used his horses on a few occasions. But where are we going?

"About another three miles further out from here there's the home of Brigadier Ramsbotham," said Polly.

"Blimey, you know the old Brigadier, ain't this world small. Innocent's told me some stories about the old Brigadier, said he was a scoundrel of the old sort, a good man through and through. He knew him when he was younger."

"We knew him when we visited the estate on days out from the orphanage. He had a massive estate and would love to take us around his maze. It is one of the largest mazes in the country and built with a mixture of yew, hornbeam and holly."

"Let's see these horses Col, sometimes I don't do well with horses. If we can't find one that will carry me, we might have to change our plans a little," said Will.

"Follow me", said Col and jogged down the road to a small house adjacent to the stables. He knocked sharply on the wooden door and stepped back. Shortly they heard the sound of shuffling feet and the door was opened to show an old man holding a gas lamp up.

"Who's there, what time do you call this to waking an honest man?" he grumbled.

"We need your help, please," said Col.

"Col, is that you? Blimey I 'aven't seen you in a while, what can I do for you this dark night?"

"Three horses Jim if you've got them, the fastest you have."

"Come with me, I've got ones that will sort you out, always 'appy to 'elp you."

The man led them through and out into a large yard at the back of his house which was lined on both sides with horseboxes. Kicking on the door of one he called out.

"Boy, get yourself up and sort out some saddles, we've got important personages 'ere. Can you 'elp 'im Col?"

"You got an 'orse that ain't afraid of big dogs, Mister?" asked Will as he passed by one horse box and the incumbent backed away baring its teeth.

"Try the one at the end, young man, 'e's so cussed in 'is character don't reckon 'e's scared of anything. Give 'im this," he said throwing a small apple to Will, "'e's a sucker for an apple."

Will walked up to the large black head of the horse and stood looking at him, holding out the apple on the flat of his hand. The horse sniffed, jerked his head back as it looked at him, took a step back, then came forward, snorted, bared its teeth but then snickered and reached forward to neatly take the apple from his hand.

"Reckon 'e'll carry you, don't you worry about it," said the old man as he went up to the box, unlatched the half door and led the horse out.

Working at speed, the old man, his boy and Col saddled the three horses and with a quick exchange of gold the back gate was opened and they were back on the road leading out of the city.

"He's going to stay outside and keep an eye out for Quinn. He'll tell him where we've gone, we don't now need to stop until we get there," said Col.

"Then lead on Polly, get us to the Brigadier's as soon as possible," said Will.

Polly clicked her heels against her horse and the three of them galloped along the road.

4 THE MAZE

Polly pulled back gently on the reins to slow down the horse beneath her. She turned to look at Col and pointed ahead of herself at a large manor house which showed as little more than a dark shadow against the night sky. Col came up alongside her.

"Is that where we are headed?" he asked.

"Not quite, the maze is in the extensive gardens. There is a small wooden outhouse, which is just outside of the maze over there, out of sight of the main house. That's where we are headed. We can leave the horses there, as there is some cover for them. However, we need to be very quiet now and proceed with caution, in case there are any lookouts keeping watch."

Alongside the road they were on ran a rough bramble filled hedge. Will got down from his horse and went over to the six barred gate that provided entrance to the field. He opened it and led his horse through, Polly and Col rode through and stopped as Will closed the gate behind and got back onto his horse.

"We'll follow the hedge round, keep in single file, the outhouse we want is just the other side of this field. We will be able to see the maze in a few moments," Polly whispered to Col.

"I hear something," said Will.

Polly and Col strained but couldn't pick up what Will's sharper hearing had heard.

"What is it Will?"

"There are men calling out to each other. They're in the maze, Polly and they're hunting something. No wait, not something, they's hunting Innocent, but somehow he's hidden himself. Seems they've lost track of him."

"Then he's still alive, quickly Will let's get to the outhouse."

They rode along to the other side of the field, where Will jumped down and opened another gate.

"We can lead the horses from here, the outhouse is just the other side of the gate," said Polly as she jumped down.

Col followed them as they led him to a small outhouse that had a small shelter built on one side. They tied the horses up underneath the shelter and went inside the outhouse.

Polly took out her lamp from a pocket and a dim light illuminated the dusty, cobwebbed filled room.

"Doesn't look like anyone's been in here for a while. With any luck they don't know about its secret," said Will.

He went over to one corner and crouched down to run his hands across the floorboards; he stopped, put his finger through a knot hole and pulled up one small section. Underneath was a metal ring, Will took hold and pulled, for a moment nothing happened and then slowly a section of the floor came up and Col could see the rungs of a ladder leading downwards.

"It hasn't been used in years Pol, he didn't find it, the Brigadier never did tell him. He said it would always be our secret that he didn't trust 'im with that bit of knowledge. Come on, we may yet be in time," Will disappeared down the hole and Polly followed after him. Col clambered down after her and crouched down to see Polly and Will already on hands and knees waiting for him.

"It's a bit smaller than I remember it," said Will.

"We were children Will, we were smaller," said Polly smiling.

The tunnel was narrow and the ceiling was so low that even Polly couldn't stand upright in it but the walls were smooth and it looked in good shape.

"Shall we?" she said and took the lead. Will and Col came after her crawling along as it was easier than trying to walk.

"This is worse than being on board a ship," said Col.

"Don't worry, it's not far," replied Will, "and it brings us up into the centre of the maze, we just have to hope the other side is still working and no one is there to welcome us."

Silence descended on the three as they made their way along the dark tunnel, muscles complaining at the misuse and cramped conditions. The air smelt of damp earth and dust and Polly had to stifle a sneeze as she worked her way along the tunnel. The floorboards that were laid along the floor were still in reasonably good shape which was testament to the skill levels of the men who had created the escape route so many years previously. Polly remembered the old Brigadier telling them stories of the uses he had made of the tunnel. She smiled at how he had sworn them both to secrecy and had made them shake his hand and promise never to use the tunnel for anything underhand or nefarious.

Finally the tunnel came to an end and she stopped and looked up. Ahead of her was another ladder that rose up out of sight.

"Do you want to see if you can get us out of here Will?"

Will moved passed her and climbed the ladder set into the wall. Polly and Col could hear him push against something and then the night air breezed across them, as Will's legs disappeared from view. Polly turned off her lamp and followed, Col came up after her.

The central folly of the maze was empty but now Polly and Col could hear what Will had already picked up. She could now hear the sound of men calling to each other across the high hedges of the maze.

"You seen him anywhere?"

"This one's giving us a good hunt."

"We'll get him, there's nowhere to hide."

"He's mine, he blacked my eye, I owe him one."

"He's still alive then," said Col with relief, "but how do we find him."

"Just as important, 'ow are we going to deal with those men out there?" asked Will, looking at Polly. "I don't reckon they's going to be too happy with us for joining the party. Are we going to play fair, don't seem right somehow though."

"They have killed already Will, I have every belief that once they discover we are here, they will do their best to kill us, they will have to attempt it at any rate. I think it is fair to say that all gloves are off; we must survive the night to bring them to justice. Even if that means killing them."

Will smiled and began to undress.

"I'll get changed then, if you can locate Innocent, we can decide which way each of us should go."

Polly stepped closer to the front of the folly and began to speak.

"In this dark night let innocence shine
A light for me to see and find
None other to see or use
As I will it so let it be."

She looked around and saw a light spring up over one part of the maze. She turned to Col.

"I've found Innocent; he's along the right-hand side of the maze. Will you go to the left. Hunt down the killers and work your way back to here. Col and I will go directly to Innocent and then do the same. Hopefully we will succeed in our rescue mission."

A small chuff of agreement came from Will and he loped off into the maze, his dark coat of fur merging into the shadows.

"Come on Col, follow me, let's go and find Innocent. We'll take the fastest route; let's not alert them to our presence until we've found him."

She walked up to the hedge in front of her, waved her hand and the dense branches swept aside allowing them to step through. Moving swiftly, stopping occasionally as they heard men close by, she led Col through the maze until she stopped and bent down to a dark shape lying half hidden beneath a hedge.

She leant down to touch the shape and was suddenly thrown backwards and a man's hand was around her throat. She reached up to his hands and gasped for air.

"Innocent, its Polly, don't hurt her," whispered Col urgently and the hands immediately let go of her throat.

"Polly, Col, how on earth? What are you doing here? We've got to get out, they'll kill us. I think I know the way back to the entrance but the devils have been tracking me too well."

"It's alright Inno, Polly's got a way out," said Col.

"It's not alright, there's ten men in this maze intent on hunting down and killing me."

As Innocent spoke a wolf's howl rang out on the night air, a man screamed and then they heard the snap of strong jaws and the sound of bones cracking and the gurgle of a throat torn out.

"What in heaven's name was that?" asked Innocent.

"That was Will, in wolf form," said Col "and I would hazard a guess there are now only nine men in this maze, though I wonder how long it will take until they realise that now they have become the hunted."

Innocent began to laugh.

"Oh how ironic, the Wolfpack Killers being hunted by a wolf. Suddenly I'm feeling much better. This night is beginning to improve," said Innocent.

Lights suddenly lit up around the maze and a voice rang out over the night air.

"To all those in the maze, you are now surrounded. My name is Detective Quinn and I assure all those that are innocent of any crime committed tonight will be allowed to walk away free when they exit the maze. To the killers of Ralph Smith and other victims yet to be identified be aware that from this point on you are all on trial for murder. From what I have just heard, it remains to be seen in what condition you emerge from this maze."

Innocent smiled at Polly.

"Now that is a rare and clever Detective, if we get out of this I will buy him the best drinks in town. He has just given us carte blanche to join the hunt. Shall we have some fun Col?"

"I am certainly up for meting out a little vengeance Inno. Can you lead us through the maze to get us back to the centre Polly, I don't think we need the fast route now," said Col, grinning.

"I can," she said and pointed to the right.

Innocent stood up as they heard Will make another kill and shouts of fear begin to ring out.

"What the bleeding hell is going on?"

"It sounds like a big dog."

"Sounds more like a bloody wolf to me."

Around the corner of the hedge a man came running and skidded to a halt as he saw Col in front of him, he turned to run but Col caught hold of him, lifted him up above his head and slammed him into the ground. The man's neck snapped on impact and his body flopped onto the ground.

"That makes seven left I believe," said Innocent, "Will is two to your one at the moment, are you going to let the wolf have all the glory my friend?"

"Stop joking about this Innocent," said Polly.

"Why. I'm sorry Polly, but they were joking about killing me, now the tables are turned. I am not the sort of man to have compassion at such a moment."

Another howl rang out and a man screamed as he died.

"Six," intoned Innocent, "I believe it should be your turn next Col, you are now three to one. Please Polly, lead us out of here, I would fain buy your detective a glass of champagne before morning comes."

Polly smiled involuntarily and pointed the next way along to Col. As they turned the corner they saw a man crouched down trying to hide inside a holly bush. Col dragged him out and flung him down on the ground. The man sprung up and stared at Col.

"Who the hell are you and what are you doing in the maze?"

"I came for my friend, you finally chose the wrong victim to hunt. Now you have me to contend with."

The man advanced towards Col and then swung a punch towards his stomach but before it could land, Col turned, took hold of the man's hand and threw him over to land heavily on the ground, screaming as his shoulder dislocated. Col reached down took the man's head in his hands and twisted, his neck cracked and the screaming stopped.

"Five, the odds are improving," said Innocent.

"Any time you want to join in Inno, it is fine with me," said Col.

"I would but I'm still extremely weary from my earlier attempts to escape this lot."

"Hmm, I'm sure you are and the fact that Polly is helping you along has nothing to do with your reluctance?"

"Nothing at all my dear friend and in any case it gives me a chance to watch a master at work. I hate to think that you have become soft with easy living."

"Easy living? I don't think working with you constitutes easy living, thank you very much," said Col as another man came running towards them, a thick branch in his hand which he swung towards Col's head.

Col simply plucked it out of his hand and as the sounds of another man dying at Will's teeth came to them, Col slammed the branch into the man's throat. He careered back hands clawing at his throat desperately trying to breathe, before Col landed a punch so hard over his heart that it stopped beating and the man fell to the floor.

"Three" said Polly dryly.

"You're getting the idea" laughed Innocent.

Col gestured for them to be quiet as he moved to the side of the walkway. A man crept round the corner and on seeing Innocent and Polly began to run towards them, without seeing Col pressed up against the high sided maze wall. As he passed Col, he put out a leg causing the man to trip and fall to the ground. Col was quickly on him and another broken neck signalled another death.

"Don't say it Innocent, we can all count. There is only one man left," said Polly as they heard Will's growls and more screams echo around the maze before stopping abruptly. "The centre of the maze is just around the corner," she added.

There was one man standing in the central clearing as they turned the corner. Polly saw Will enter from the other side and he wagged his tail in greeting.

"Seems we counted correctly," said Innocent, as he raised himself up from leaning on Polly's shoulder. "If you would all be so kind, I would like to deal with this one myself."

"Do you know who he is then Inno?" asked Col.

"Yes, he is the head of this pack which he so grandly called the Wolfpack. But it was me that cost him that little finger and I still have the measure of him."

"Will and I know him as well Innocent, earlier than you as he still had all his fingers then," said Polly.

"You do? You must enlighten me at a later date. Now though I believe it is time to finish this evening's entertainment."

He stepped forward as Will began to inch forward from the other side; a low growl emanating from his throat.

The man backed away from Will and called out to Innocent.

"Call your dog off, Jack. Unless you feel you need his backup to take me down. But be careful I've learnt a lot since you last saw me."

"As have I, I am not the man I was then. However, I believe that whilst I have changed, you are fundamentally still a coward."

The man snarled and came towards Innocent, as he stepped away from Polly and went forward to meet him.

The man's first punch missed, as Innocent weaved away and came back in to slam a punch into the man's stomach. He doubled over in pain but Innocent pulled him up and sent a fist towards the man's chin, the blow sending the man flying backwards.

Getting slowly to his feet he shook his head clear it and came back in. This time Innocent traded punches with him, wicked blows opened up cuts to their faces and their breath came quickly as their strength waned.

"He's a fool, he can't win this way, what's he doing, step out Inno, step out," said Col under his breath.

Innocent must have heard him or come to the same realisation himself because he suddenly moved backwards avoiding a punch to his head.

"Had enough Jack," sneered the man but Innocent just smiled.

The man backed up, raised his arms once more and as Innocent stepped forward; the man threw out a feint, followed by a strong left punch which would have finished Innocent had it landed. But Innocent didn't take the feint; instead he weaved away, ducked beneath the left punch and threw a short vicious jab to the man's rib, which cracked on impact. The man grunted in pain but couldn't move out of the way quick enough to avoid Innocent's second jab that pushed the broken rib further into his body. He stepped back, put his hand over his ribs, pain showing on his face as he looked at Innocent.

"No more, I'm done, I'm sorry, please don't hurt me anymore I can't take it, please, Jack please, for the friendship we had" he begged.

"Jack's dead, and we were never friends," said Innocent as he stepped back, turned and sent his foot slamming into the man's side, crushing the small bones of his hand holding his side and pushing the broken ribs further into his body. The force of the kick sent him flying backwards screaming in pain as blood bubbled up and out of his mouth. He gasped for air but nothing could save him, he died as his lungs filled up with blood.

Innocent stood looking down at him breathing heavily, took two steps back and fell into Col as he came up to him.

"You could have finished that much earlier, why did you fight like that."

"I wanted him to feel what his victims had felt; he had no right to die easily."

"He certainly didn't die easily. You are a hard man Innocent," said Polly.

"I don't kill people for sport, Polly. I despise those who prey on those weaker than them. He was always a bully who only fought when he was sure of the outcome, I should have finished him the night I severed his finger. But I was a different man then and it was a long time ago", he looked at Polly "you said you knew him, how?"

"When Will and I were in the orphanage as children, the old Brigadier used to let all of us come and play here; that man was his grandson. He would take the younger kids into the maze promising them sweets but would then run away and leave them lost in the maze. Will and I went into the maze by ourselves and learnt our way round the whole thing so that we could hide in there and then guide the younger ones out after he had run away and left them frightened and confused. When the Brigadier found out what we were doing he showed us the tunnel out through the central folly and told us to keep it secret, even from his grandson. That old man knew the boy was no good but there was nothing he could do about it. It certainly doesn't sound as interesting as your story; will you tell me more?"

"It's too long a story for now, a different time, a different me. Time now to go and meet your Detective I think, but I could do with a short rest," he said as he sat down heavily on the ground and leaned against the wall of the folly.

Will came across and leant against Polly, his muzzle was sticky with blood and she could see where blood had matted the fur on his body.

"It has been a hard night, let us all take a few minutes before we head out. If we take more time than that we will have Gadget storming in to try to find us. Go and change Will, get dressed and then we can help Innocent up and out of this maze, if you still remember the way?" said Polly.

Will growled gently and pushed against her leg a bit before stalking away from her and going into the folly.

When he came back out he leant down and helped Innocent to stand up.

"Shall we get out of here Innocent, I for one am getting hungry. It's not easy holding myself back when there is so much delectable food on offer," he said looking across at the dead man and licking his lips.

"Would you, really, I mean really?" asked Innocent pushing himself upright and backing away from Will.

Polly laughed. "Stop teasing him Will, he's had a hard night. Of course he wouldn't Innocent. Well not unless he was really starving."

"You're too easy to fool Innocent; I like my food well cooked, don't you worry. Come on, let's get out of here and let Quinn take over."

He turned and set of down one of the paths leading away from the folly and within a very short space of time he led them all to the main entrance where they found Quinn and Gadget standing alone.

"I thought you said the maze was surrounded, Quinn, where's all your men?" said Will looking around but seeing no one else.

"I did say the maze was surrounded, I just didn't say by what. Your young assistant is remarkably resourceful, lights rigged all around the maze in minutes; certainly she did enough to convince those inside it that they were surrounded by men. Hopefully we did enough to aid you in there." He patted Gadget on the shoulder in appreciation as she beamed with pride.

"Told you I was good, didn't I Detective Quinn?" she said.

"That you did young lady and I was suitably impressed," he looked at Polly, "is it done?" he added solemnly.

"It's done," said Polly, "the men that killed Ralph have paid for their crimes."

"Whilst I'm not upset that none of them have walked out with you, some proof of their guilt would help in my writing up the case."

"I can get you the proof," said Innocent, stepping around Polly and looking at Quinn.

"Ah Mr Innocent, I don't believe I've had the pleasure of being introduced to you before, I'm Detective Alec Quinn."

Quinn stepped forward and put out his hand. Innocent stared at him for a moment and then put out his hand and shook Quinn's.

"Good to meet you Sir and thank you for your assistance. I would be proud to buy you a drink in thanks once we have left this place. But first the proof, if you will come with me up to the main house, there is a book. It lists their kills. My name was to be entered on the next line once they had dispatched me. I warn you now it is a large book."

Polly stepped up to Innocent and he leant on her shoulder as the small party walked up to the stone staircase leading to the main door of the old manor house just as daylight began to creep across the night sky.

As they got to the top of the staircase Polly looked back over her shoulder at the maze that was now quiet and still in the early morning light. A shiver ran through her as she thought of what might have happened.

Innocent looked down at her.

"Thank you Polly, it could have been very different. You have saved me once more. The debt I owe you is growing. It means a lot that you came for me."

"I didn't do it just for you Innocent. I did it for Col and all the victims in that book. You do not owe me anything. I'm just glad we all survived."

"It is to be celebrated Polly. Would you consent to my requesting the pleasure of your company one evening so that I can say thank you in more pleasant surroundings than a dark, dangerous maze?"

Polly looked up at him and smiled.

"An evening out with a rogue? I think I could manage that."

"Come then, let me show Quinn the book and we will all get home and be able to rest."

"That would be nice," said Polly, "I could do with an uninterrupted night's sleep, even if I start it in the morning!"

THE TAKEOVER BID
AFFAIR

1 EARLY EVENING

Innocent tapped on the roof of the Cab and the cabbie smoothly brought his team to a halt outside the impressive fronting of the oldest restaurant in London. He waited for the cabbie to get down and open the door before stepping elegantly out of the cab. He reached up to take Polly's hand and help her down the cab's pull-out step, then turned to the cabbie and passed over a coin.

"Thank you Bert, a very smooth journey, we'll be walking back so don't worry about looking for us later."

"Very good, Mr Innocent, you 'ave a good evening, I 'ear the food is bloody marvellous in there."

"It was the last time I was here, many moons ago now. I trust it will be so again tonight."

Bert pocketed the gold coin, tipped his cap to Innocent with a smile and a wink. He climbed back up onto his high perch and settled himself into place. He picked up the reins, clicked to his horses and with a final wave of his hand, his cab moved smoothly away.

"Bert always was a show off, but he is the smoothest ride in this city," said Innocent, turning to Polly. He smiled as he saw her confusion. "What's wrong Polly, do you not approve of my choice of dining establishment?"

He looked at the plain simple door, behind which he knew lay the richly decorated interior and exquisite menu that rightfully held a high place in the dining choices of the aristocracy.

"We can't be going in here, Innocent, I know you said you wanted to thank me after what happened in the maze but this is too much, I could never afford to come here."

"Then it's a good job that I can afford it isn't it and I do not believe that I have ever intimated that you would be paying for this evening. This is my way of saying thank you for saving my life on two occasions. Now don't worry about a thing, they know me here and we will have a good reception I promise."

Polly looked around at Covent Garden. Christmas was on its way and the area was lit up with decorations. Stalls were laid out selling all manner of goods. The area had been cleaned of sewage, though a faint reminder of it sat below the rich smell of meat pies, roasting chestnuts and dried oranges. People from the highest level of society, dressed in rich velvets, furs and jewels wandered along, oblivious of the ragged children that followed behind, hoping to beg a penny or maybe pick a pocket.

She subconsciously smoothed down her skirt, feeling awkward in her less opulent attire. She had decided on a deep red skirt and high collared shirt; her corset was in a darker hue with brass chains and charms decorating its front and back. Whilst she knew she did not look too out of place, still she could hardly boast of such money as was being displayed by the other people in their attire. Innocent took her hand, raised it to his mouth and lightly kissed her knuckles.

"Polly, you are far and away the most beautiful woman here tonight, do not judge yourself alongside the vapidity that is on show. You are strong and real and the only woman I want to spend any time with. Please know that I am proud to have you as a friend and honoured that you would agree to join me tonight."

"Stop buttering me up Innocent. I know what I am and I know at what level of society I feel comfortable. I doubt any woman in that restaurant would happily walk into a maze, full of killers, after you, or tell you exactly what she thinks of you. I just do not feel that I will be regarded well in there."

"You don't accept the truth about yourself very often, do you?"

"I know the truth, I'm an orphan who grew up fighting other people's judgement of me; now I have a chance to make something of myself and to be honest, your friendship might, and I hesitate over the might, cause me difficulties if I wish to rise above my station. However, I enjoy your company enough to not allow it to worry me overly at this present time. Now, are we actually going to enter this establishment or continue to chatter on the pavement in the cold?"

Innocent smiled at her as he held his arm out. Polly placed her hand on his arm and let him lead her up to the entrance.

The doorman, tall and stern in his demeanour, resplendent in brocade trimmed morning suit and top hat reached out to open the door for them. As he turned to greet them he saw Innocent and a broad grin ruined his professional attitude.

"My Lord," he said "It has been too long since you have graced us with your presence. I trust nothing untoward has kept you from our doors?"

"Nothing that needs worry you Charles, I have simply been working too hard in making my own world in this town to have the time to visit you."

"Then it is good to see you back and I assure you nothing here has changed. Enjoy your meal."

"Thank you Charles, it is good to see you." Innocent led Polly in through the door and it closed smoothly behind them.

"My Lord?" said Polly but Innocent just smiled and said nothing.

He led her to the cloakroom area, removed his cape and top hat and handed them over to the girl. He then turned to help Polly, only to find she was already passing over her cape and small hat to the girl.

"You really don't like anyone helping you, do you?" he said.

Polly just smiled at him and said, "Where do we go now?"

Innocent took her hand and led her through to the entrance of the dining room. The suave maître de came towards them and then as he saw Innocent a grin to rival Charles' came on his face.

"My Lord, how wonderful of you to come, I hardly dared hope you would actually be visiting us when I saw your name on our booking sheet. You look well, My Lord," he turned to look at Polly and only by a tiny crease in his forehead did she realise that he wasn't sure he approved of her, but he still turned back to Innocent and asked, "who is this enchanting lady with you?"

"Jean-Paul, this is my very dear friend, Pollyanne Baker, she recently saved my life so I thought to bring her to my favourite restaurant to say thank you."

Jean-Paul looked at Polly again and this time he did not quickly glance away and she saw the change in his eyes as he realised that his summation of her based on her outward appearance was incorrect. He smiled at her and she felt that he was being genuine towards her.

"Saved your life, my Lord, my goodness, well then my dear you are most welcome to our humble establishment and I trust our offerings will be sufficient payment."

"May we have a table away from the main floor, Jean-Paul? Whilst I am happy to be here, I would not want to be the subject of too much chatter amongst the other patrons. It has been a long time since I have been abroad in such society."

"Of course, my Lord, come this way, I have the perfect spot already prepared for you."

Jean-Paul turned and led them to a table which was set back from the open main area. It was almost totally enclosed by the high-backed red velvet covered circular seating. Polly slid into one side as Innocent sat down opposite her.

"I shall bring you the menu for this evening shortly, my Lord but in the meantime, would you like something to drink, I do have rather a special red wine available this evening."

"That would be lovely Jean-Paul but could you also bring us some fresh water, I do not drink in the same way as I used to. I will not be falling out of your establishment as I was prone to do before."

"That is good to hear my Lord, though you used to fall so elegantly as I recall." He smiled, looked around and clicked his fingers to a hovering waiter. The man nodded, turned on his heel and disappeared through a door.

"If you require anything you have only to ask, My Lord. And I hope you don't mind if I add, that it is most pleasing to see you again." Jean-Paul left them and went back to his place near the entrance in time to welcome a new set of customers into the restaurant.

"They seem to know you well here Innocent."

"It was a long time ago Polly, I was younger and more reckless with my life than I am now. I was not always Mr Innocent, resident of Soho and proprietor of The Hangman's Dance. At one point I was the younger son, with no responsibility and a real sense of not belonging. Hence the falling out of this place at regular intervals."

The waiter returned with a heavy bottomed glass carafe filled with a rich red wine. He poured a little bit into Innocent's glass and waited for his approving nod before pouring a measure into both their glasses. Another waiter appeared with a carafe filled with water which he placed on the table along with two small glass tumblers.

Innocent sipped his wine and motioned for Polly to do the same; she picked up the delicate glass and took a small sip. The rich red wine tasted wonderful, bringing her the suggestion of oak barrels and blackcurrants to her taste buds.

"I've never tasted red wine like this before, is this what you were used to, when you were younger."

"It is a good vintage and yes I used to be partial to such as this but enough about me, tell me a bit about your childhood. From the way you work with Will I am guessing you have known him for a long time. I admit that I worry I am stepping on his toes this evening."

Polly smiled, "Will and I aren't like that, Innocent and it is true I have known Will for years, the whole of my life in fact. We grew up together in an orphanage, neither knowing where we had come from or who we would turn out to be. What is between us is an understanding that comes from shared experiences and facing up to the differences between us and the others around us."

"For example your magic and his, to put it politely, shape changing ability."

"Yes, discovering those as we grew up was challenging. I learnt a lot about my skills as I helped Will to manage his. It's hard to hide a wolf in a dormitory when you are watched almost constantly; you very quickly learn coping strategies."

Jean-Paul arrived at their table and presented the menu.

"The duck is superb this evening and I can also recommend the fish."

Innocent took the menu and began to consider the options.

###

Will looked around at the empty bar room. Without customers it seemed a little strange, as though it was waiting for something to happen. The mirrors behind the long bar caught the reflections of the lamps outside the building through the tall leaded windows and he could hear the creak of the sign at the front of the inn as the wind caught it and swung it back and forth. The fire was lit in the hearth and lamps were lit around the table he was sat at with Col and Gadget. They had been playing cards for a while and he had yet to catch Gadget out. He was well aware that Col hadn't even worked out that she was cheating. There was a large pile of matchsticks in front of Gadget, a smaller one in front of him and Col was down to his last few.

Col looked down at the cards in his hand and grimaced.

"I would swear that something is not quite right here. I have been unlucky all evening."

Will laughed. "Why do you think we are only playing for matchsticks Col, if Gadget wants to play, money is always off the table."

Col stared at Gadget disbelieving that such a small girl could have manipulated the cards without him noticing.

"Sorry Col but I like to keep my 'and in, sometimes it's too 'ard not to work the cards in my favour."

"No wonder you succeeded in your life of petty crime, you look so innocent and guileless."

"It has certainly served me well. Could you tell me the time Col?"

Col reached to his pocket for his watch and grimaced as he realised his pocket was empty. He looked up to see Gadget grinning from ear to ear and dangling his watch from her out stretched hand.

"She's incorrigible sometimes, we do our best to teach her better ways but it's easy to take the child out of the streets but you can't always take the streets out of the child," said Will.

"Aw Will, you know I don't thieve no more but in our line of business it's useful to keep up my skills, Polly picks locks doesn't she? And aren't I giving 'im his watch back?" said Gadget.

Col laughed and took the watch back.

"Lesson learnt little one, I shall be more careful of my belongings around you and see if I can't catch you out with the cards."

"You'll be better than me if you can" said Will "sometimes it's only my nose that will pick up if she's cheating, she gets excited if she's managed to pull one over you and whilst I can't see it on her face, I can smell it on 'er."

Col looked at him. "You can smell excitement?"

"I can smell most emotions, but it's hard to explain what they smell like. Everyone smells different, but it's very useful if I want to find out if someone is lying. As a wolf I get excited if I smell fear, it starts the hunt. I've just worked on that to use it in my human form."

Col considered him and smiled. "You are a dangerous man to know Will Dagger, I'm glad that I can call you friend."

"Likewise Col, I would not wish to come up against you, Polly told me how you dealt with the men in the maze."

"Let us not discuss that Will, tonight is not a night for such remembrances. So Gadget, my question to you would be when and why did you decide to go straight?" said Col.

"That was Polly, Col. It came as a shock I can tell you, I was the best, I hadn't ever been caught. I was the quickest at getting in and getting out, but just when I thought I was going to manage it again, there was Polly, standing there looking at me and I knew I was done for," said Gadget.

"Polly caught 'er one day trying to get in Mr Hardaker's shop, gave 'er a choice, come and work for us or get 'anded over to the peelers and sent overseas for robbery."

"I didn't much fancy the idea of surviving in the stinking belly of a ship for months and when I had a good fink about the whole thing, to be totally truthful Col, I was getting a bit fed up of living off me wits and spending most of me time 'ungry. When Polly offered me the chance to go straight, it weren't that difficult a decision to make. Now I 'ave as much fun as I did when I were younger but it feels like I'm doing good and 'elping people. I sleep better at night and it's not just cause I've a bed and a roof over me head."

"What about you Will? When did you and Polly get together? I'm surprised that you are happy for Inno to take her out for a meal, you know he is attracted to her?"

"Polly's not mine in that way Col, we aren't that inclined to each other. We grew up together in a hard place; orphanages aren't renowned for their comfortable living standards. We started to change as we grew older and facing the world together gave us the courage to look for a way out. I reckon Polly would have made it but I know I wouldn't have without 'er. She can do what she likes Col, I wouldn't reckon on messing up anything she wanted to do. She knows I'm here for 'er, no matter what."

"Still, it must be a little strange?"

"Don't worry your 'ead about it Col," said Gadget "with those two it's like a 'abit for 'em. I gave up trying to understand 'ow they can come up with the same answer to a problem from two different angle ages ago. I just reckon myself lucky that they keep me around."

"When did you meet Innocent?" said Will.

Col's face darkened a little.

"If you don't want to tell me, it's fine" said Will, "Things you don't want to remember is understandable."

"No, you have a right to know, you have graced me with the truth of who and what you are. It is only right if I offer you the same in return. I grew up a long way away from this country, in a land where the sun always shone. If I walked out of my front door I would see nothing but empty land for miles. Then men came to our village and took all the young boys and women. They killed anyone who tried to stop them. Thankfully my father was out in the fields working; otherwise I'm sure he would have been killed. One day I will go back and tell him that I survived when many of those taken did not and found a grave at the bottom of the sea."

"You must 'ate it 'ere, it's always cold 'n dark 'n smelly," said Gadget.

"No, I don't hate it here, little one, I was lucky; Inno found me and took me from my slavery."

"What gave you the scars?" said Will.

"Growing up on the ship you had to fight for any food, I got good at fighting. When I grew too big to work on a ship I was sold to a man who ran a fight tournament where to survive you had to fight. Sometimes the only way to survive another day was to kill your opponent. I am not proud of my life but when you have been beaten down so low that you know nothing different but the straw you lie down on at night and the circle you enter the next day, well you become nothing more than a sewer rat, fighting to see another dawn."

"And I thought the orphanage was tough, I don't know I would 'ave got through that and come out like you did Col," said Will.

"If Inno hadn't wandered into the tent one day I doubt I would have Will. But he saw something in me that made him go over to the slaver and pay him enough for my freedom. I have been by his side ever since. He never judged me for what I had done, just gave me the chance to remake myself into a man I hope my father would be proud of."

"I reckon any man would be proud to 'ave you as a son Col," said Will. Then he cocked his head to one side and a look of concentration came over his face.

"Are you expecting a large body of people to be coming this way this evening?" asked Will.

"No, the inn is closed, all the regulars know that. He did it so he could take Polly somewhere nice. But he does this once in a while in any case to give the girls some time off to relax and see family. Why?"

"Cause there's a large group of people coming this way and they are doing their best to stay very quiet. I would hazard a guess that they aren't friendly visitors."

2 LATE EVENING

Polly sighed with regret as she finished off the final mouthful of the dark chocolate mousse that she had in front of her. The meal had been unlike anything she had ever tasted before. Each course had been presented on simple white plates with the food beautifully displayed. The flavours of each course had been exciting and new to her palate. She was sure she would always remember the first time she had tasted such wonderful food.

"Did you enjoy that?" asked Innocent.

"It was perfect, I don't think I have ever tasted something so rich before in my life. To think some people eat like this every day."

"Yes they do and in doing so they lose the ability to appreciate it. Much better to only partake of such richness occasionally that way you can fully indulge and know how truly magnificent it is."

"Then I will try to remember this evening for as long as I can, it has been a glimpse into another way of life, one that I do not believe I will ever be a part of."

"Neither should you wish to Polly, my dear. I assure you I ran from it and not a day goes by without me knowing that I would do anything I could to ensure I don't ever go back. The people are, in general, cruel and heartless. They are accustomed to getting their way in all things, they believe that money will get them everything they desire and they see no reason to consider how their actions might impact on those they perceive to be beneath them. Such as you and I, Col, Will and Gadget are nothing and are to be treated as such. They do not see the good that can be found in the gutter."

"Surely not all are like that, you weren't, otherwise why would you have been so welcomed here this evening?"

"Ah but I was always aware of my position and I hated it. Therefore when I saw the workers of this world I understood the trials that life brought them. I was always chastised for my easy relationship with such people. But I like to believe it helps me now in my line of business."

"One day you must tell me how you came into your business, what turned you away from here, what happened to the second son that he became Mr Innocent."

"One day I may, but it is not a good story and I would be loath to ruin such a night as we have had with the sordid details of my fall from grace."

"Very well, maybe it is time for us to go. I do not want to keep Gadget up too late and she is still only a child."

"Please do not be angry with me Polly."

"I'm not angry Innocent, there are parts of my life that I would not wish to share. It has been a wonderful evening but such richness for one unused to such is tiring. I would not wish to fall asleep in front of you. I think a walk back to the inn before the lights go out would be lovely."

"There are not many women who would walk the streets openly with me. It is a dry night, though a little cold but it was an indulgence to arrive here by cab, so we will not be in the cold for too long. Let me just settle up with Jean-Paul and we can be on our way."

Innocent stood up, bowed to her and left the booth and made his way towards the main entrance. Polly watched as he talked with Jean-Paul, she noticed how many of the other diners glanced in his direction and then turned back to their table and pointed to him discreetly and whispered to their companions. She wondered what they were all saying about him. It was tempting to try and listen in to their chatter but the evening was perfect as it was. She knew enough about Innocent to know why she was there and did not need to spoil things by eavesdropping into gossip.

Innocent came back to the table and reached out a hand to help her from her seat. He led her out through the tables and back to the cloakroom where he took her cloak from the girl before Polly could reach it. He smiled as he placed it gently around her shoulders and handed her hat to her, before taking his own cape and swirling it elegantly around his shoulders and placing his top hat on his head.

Charles opened the door for them as they got close and inclined his head to them both.

"I trust you had a good meal and were not disturbed in any way."

"It was perfect as always Charles and a pleasure to return."

"I trust you will not leave so long a gap of time before visiting us again?"

"Such richness as this should be savoured Charles and visited only on special occasions."

"A wise decision my Lord. Good night to you both and it was good to see you so well my Lord."

"A good night to you to Charles."

Innocent turned towards Soho and Polly linked her arm in his and they started to walk back towards The Hanged Man.

"Were you really a Lord then?"

"History Polly, a title I never wanted and certainly never deserved. But there is no way to stop them applying it to me. To most of London I am Mr Innocent now and happy in my skin. I can cope with them calling me by that ridiculous title because I know they use it in fondness and not as an accusation."

Polly looked at the pocket watch she kept in her corset.

"I had not realised it was quite so late. I hope that Gadget has behaved herself tonight, she can be handful at times."

"Do not worry about her or Will, Col will see that they are safe and I'm sure they have plenty of things to occupy them. I believe Col was going to bring out a pack of cards."

Polly laughed.

"Then I hope Will insisted on playing for matchsticks, Gadget cannot play any card game without cheating. If the three of us ever play, the aim of the game is not to win but to catch her out."

Innocent laughed and went to say something but a group of men came out of the darkness of an alley next to them and surrounded them.

"What do you want, we don't have any money for you to steal and I promise we are not a weak mark," said Innocent.

One of the men smiled at him and before Polly could react Innocent crumpled to the floor next to her. In concentrating on the men in front of them and still full of the evening's enjoyment neither of them had kept up with their normal observation of their surroundings. The billy club wielded by the man behind them landed before either was aware of him.

"Get rid of the girl, we don't want any witnesses to this," said the man in front. Polly was grabbed and could sense the man reaching for his knife.

Frantically she sent out a thought, mouthing the words silently to ensure they took effect as soon as possible.

"You need me; he will be more easy to deal with if he thinks you will hurt his lady friend. Bring her along for the ride; she will regret being his friend before the night is out."

The look on the leader's face changed.

"Stop," he said. "Finking abawt it, bring 'er along, 'aving 'er along might keep 'im behaving as we want."

The man changed his grip on Polly, lifting her off the ground and carrying her along as two men reached down to Innocent, grabbed him under his arms and dragged him along to the end of the alley. As they got to the end, a cab pulled up and they were thrown in before Polly could even utter a sound. Polly noticed there were no windows available and no light sources just as the door clanged shut behind them and she was left with the comatose Innocent.

She was lying on the floor of the cab next to Innocent so she felt her way along his torso up to his throat. Under her fingers she felt his pulse beat out strongly and breathed a sigh of relief.

"At least they do not mean to kill you yet then. We may still get out of this alive but it is not the way I wished this evening to end. I hope that Will and Col are alright and this is not an attack aimed at your business my dear Innocent."

She sat down next to Innocent and was just beginning to consider a suitable spell to get them out of the carriage when she started to feel very tired. She realised the slight hiss she had heard was the sound of gas being pumped in to the cab. But before she could start a defence against it, she fell into the darkness and blacked out.

"Are they getting closer, can you pick up anything about them?" asked Col.

Will went to the door of the Inn and sniffed the air. "We've probably got about fifteen minutes before they get to us. They aren't moving at speed."

"We have time to make ready then. Gadget, you run upstairs, knock on all the doors and tell the girls who are there that they need to secure their rooms and then get out via the cellars. I don't want any harm to come to them. Then you follow them as I have no desire to see you harmed either."

Gadget didn't argue, just nodded and ran for the stairs, disappearing up them at top speed.

"Will, you go round this floor and close all the shutters, they all have iron bars to secure them, it will be difficult for anyone to get in and surprise us. Bar the door as well but leave this window free, I want to see who is wanting to attack us."

"Do you have anything we can defend ourselves with? I could change and go hunting if you think it would help?"

Col looked at him for a moment and then shook his head.

"No, I would rather have you here with me, especially if you know how to shoot."

"I do, though I 'aven't 'ad to for a long while."

"I will lock up downstairs and bring up the weapons from there, you will find another gun cabinet behind the bar area. I believe we will have enough fire power to make any attackers stop and think."

Col disappeared down the stairs as Will went around the inn pulling all the tall wooden shutters across the windows and putting the iron bars in the slots provided. He found the gun cabinet and smiled as he saw the collection of muskets and pistols available. Certainly the only problem would be the speed at which they could reload. There was only the two of them and from the sounds coming to his acute hearing they would be facing a considerable force of men and more men meant more rounds being fired.

He pulled all the guns out and brought them to a table near the window that Col had said to leave open. He looked up as Gadget came back down the stairs closely followed by five women.

"This is everyone who was upstairs, seems most girls 'ad gone to visit their partners or family this evening."

"What's happening?" asked one of the women to Col as he emerged from the cellars laden down with more guns.

"We are under attack, I don't know who from or why but I want you out of here and safe, so go down and out through the cellars, then you should be able to get beyond the attackers."

The woman looked at the other four and they each nodded to her in turn.

"We're not going anywhere, we all know how to fire a gun and two of you won't be able to hold out for too long."

"This isn't a fight for you, get out whilst you can," said Col.

A slender girl stepped forward.

"You don't understand Col, Innocent's a good man and working for him is easier and more profitable than any other situation we would find ourselves in. He would fight for us, so we will fight for him. You need us, Rachel and I can load the guns. Maeve, Tilly and Jane know how to shoot. That gives you five to defend this place, rather than just the two of you."

"Thank you Ruth," said Col.

"Then I'm staying as well," said Gadget.

"No," said Will, "I need to you to get out and get some 'elp. You could go and get Quinn, 'e would probably be able to bring some fire power down to us."

Gadget stood there for a bit and then grinned. "I can go and get some 'elp but I reckon I know a better group to go to than Quinn and 'is Peelers."

Before Will could ask who, she was racing away, her footsteps echoing on the stairs as she went into the cellars and then the sound faded away and she was gone.

"Right then, let's wait and see who it is that thinks they have the power to take over Inno's power base," said Col. Picking up a musket he went to the window and opened it so he had a clear view over the square in front of the Inn.

"Will, you go to one of the windows at the back and take Rachel with you; she can load for you if required. Maeve and Tilly you open the shutters for the window next to me, one of you reload for the other and Ruth you can load for me. Jane, I need you to keep your eyes open for anyone sneaking round the back and keep Will knowing what is happening here. Ready everyone?"

Maeve looked at him and smiled tightly. "Let's make sure they regret coming here tonight."

"Here they come," said Col as torch light flickered in the alleyways leading into the square. About ten men came out of each alleyway pushing a cart in front of them. They formed a semi-circle in front of the Inn and tipped over the carts, giving themselves protection from any direct fire.

"What do you want?" said Col.

One of the men stepped out from the protection of the carts and raised his torch up.

"We want you to come out peaceful like. If you do, we will escort you out of Soho and no harm will come to any of you."

"And if we don't?"

The man gestured around him.

"I reckon we outnumber you by a lot, so if you don't we're coming in and it will go 'ard on any of you who resist."

"I don't think Mr Innocent will be very pleased with us if we did not attempt to defend his home," said Col.

"Mr Innocent is dead."

A gasp from one of the women came from behind Col. Will shook his head in disbelief.

"That I will not believe until you bring me his body, until such time I will continue to fight you," said Col.

"He's been disappeared mate; no-one will ever find 'im. I promise you that my crew will not have let me down. They will have grabbed 'im and 'e will be dead and gone by dawn."

"He 'asn't mentioned Polly", said Will as he came up next to Col. "I would bet on 'er getting the two of them out of anything this lout could arrange."

"Would you know if any harm had come to her?"

"In the same way as you know right now that Innocent is still alive?"

"Then we fight?"

"I don't reckon they would really escort us out of Soho nicely if we all walked out of here with our arms raised, do you?"

"No, I don't. But I want you all to agree to my action before I answer him. Are we prepared to fight and maybe die tonight?"

All faces turned to Col and the unanimous answer came back, "We fight."

Col turned back to the window and called out "Make your move then Mister, we will fight and wait for Innocent to return."

The man smiled and melted back into the body of his group. They all raised their guns and as the defenders ducked down below the windows bullets smashed through the glass panes and buried themselves in the bar and walls.

3 THE EARLY HOURS

Polly opened her eyes and sighed in relief. At least the gas hadn't been poisonous, there was still a chance they could get out of whatever situation she and Innocent had been dragged into.

Her head ached and her thoughts were still sluggish but she realised that her eyes were beginning to be able to focus and see a little in the gloom. Light filtered down through the gaps between planks forming the ceiling above. She realised that she was lying on a damp wooden floor that smelt of dead fish. She tried to move her arms to get herself up from the floor but they were restrained behind her and the bite of rope against her skin made her wince in pain. She attempted to move her legs and found they were tied too. She struggled and wriggled around until she managed to get herself sitting upright, where at least she wasn't so close to the smell.

"Where are we I wonder'" she thought to herself. A groan of pain reached her from the darkness and she called out softly, "Innocent?"

"Polly? Is that you? Its pitch bloody black, what happened? Where are we? Bloody hell my head hurts."

"Yes, it's me and I don't know exactly where we are though I have a good idea of what we are in. Though the question remains, who have you annoyed?"

"Me? Why blame me? I'm sure you must have some disgruntled clients from your investigations," said Innocent with another groan of pain.

"Really Innocent, I'm a simple private investigator, not a crime lord like you."

"Simple! You're a powerful witch with a werewolf business partner. I don't know why someone wants to bash my head in. Why didn't you spring into action with a spell to rescue us?"

"You'd already been bundled into the carriage and they were thinking about killing me. The best I could do was to convince them to bring me along. Thankfully who ever ordered them to waylay you obviously wanted you alive."

"We may still be dead before morning. I'm trussed up like a Christmas goose, how about you?

"I'm tied up as well but not too tightly, give me a moment and I'll get to the knife I have concealed in my corset."

"Bloody hell woman, why do have a knife in your corset? We were out for a meal celebrating in the best restaurant in London. Did you think they wouldn't provide you with enough cutlery?" said Innocent.

"I always have a knife, some picklocks and other Gadget made items concealed within the lining and decoration on my corset; you never know what will come in useful in my line of work."

"Can't you just whisper a few magic words to get the rope to unravel or disintegrate?"

"Don't be silly Inno, I could use a spell and if I can't get to my knife I will. But I always carry a knife with me, just in case I'm in a situation where I can't use my magic. Also magic is tiring and I have a feeling we are going to need all our energy to get out of here, wherever here is. You should be glad I do carry a knife, you would be in right pickle if I hadn't."

Polly moved her bound hands along the back of her corset until she felt the hook at the bottom of one of the wide stays. Tugging on it began to pull out a small thin blade. As it drew clear from her corset she began to cut into the ropes around her wrists. Soon the last strand gave way and she brought her hands round to her front and eased her shoulders out a little before she leant down and began to work on the rope around her ankles.

"Why does it always seem that you are rescuing me? A lesser man might take that as an insult," said Innocent.

"A lesser man might not have been captured in the first place. Your position as the arch criminal is not looking too good at the moment."

"Cruel Polly, I will blame the whole situation on you, if you had not looked so delectable in your attire this evening, maybe I would have been able to stay aware of my surroundings. Mind you if I knew you were carrying a knife I might have felt differently about the decorations on your corset."

Polly cut through the last of the rope around her ankles and wriggled her feet to bring the feeling back into them.

"Well, I'm now free of my bindings; shall I provide us with a little light?"

"Don't tell me you have a candle and some matches hidden in your corset."

"Don't worry I have something better than a candle." Polly whispered two words and a ball of light rose up above her and lit up the small space.

She looked around herself and over towards where Innocent lay trussed up even more than she had been. She winced as she saw a trickle of blood that had dried on his face. He smiled at her and winced again with pain.

"A ship's hold, bloody hell, I hate ships. I guess it makes sense, take me out to sea, dump me over the side and I would be gone with no evidence of what had happened."

"We aren't moving so I guess we've had another stroke of luck; the tide is with us."

She pulled herself free of all the rope that she had cut away and crawled over to Innocent. She began to cut through the ropes around his wrists.

"They weren't going to take any chances with your body being found," she said as she looked down and saw that the rope around his ankles was attached to a heavy iron anchor. Innocent stretched out his shoulders as Polly cut through the rope binding him and began to work on the rope around his legs and ankles.

"Not a nice end, I've a feeling someone doesn't like me and reckoned on making me suffer in my death. Silly, should have just done the deed and got it over and done with. Will the villains never learn? But whoever ordered us to be abducted has made their first mistake. They should have had us killed in that alley. I wonder where that someone is now?"

"If I had to guess, on his way to attack your Inn," said Polly.

"Hmm, with me here, they might think it an easy target."

"But Will is there."

"So is Col."

"They are certainly not an easy pair to defeat," said Polly as she finished cutting Innocent free of all the rope around him.

"I would still like to get back there as soon as possible. Shall we make a stab at getting out of here then?" said Innocent, "thank you Polly that feels much better. I've never been one for restraints."

"If we can get out of here without alerting anyone to us leaving that would be nice. I'm not in the habit of causing harm if I can help it."

"I'm with you on that one Polly, don't worry. Most of the men on this ship will simply be following orders; I want to meet the organ grinder, not the monkeys. Shall we get moving?"

"Let me just take off my skirt, it's ruined beyond mending already."

"Do we have time for that Polly? Not that I haven't had a few fantasies about seeing you in your underwear, but I never pictured it happening in a place like this."

"Don't be silly Inno, if we need to move fast it will be easier to do it without worrying that my skirt is going to get caught in anything. I don't have this problem with Will."

"Do you often take off your skirt around him?" asked Innocent.

"Regularly."

"I'm beginning to really hate your werewolf."

Innocent turned away and began to look around for a way out of the ship's hold as Polly undid the lacing at the back of her skirt and let it fall to the floor. He gasped as he looked back at her.

"Black bloomers. You're wearing black bloomers woman. Since when was that the fashion?"

"Since I have had too many times when I've had to lose my skirt in order to escape. Will and I have led an interesting life I told you. White shows up in the dark, black does not. It became easier to make all my bloomers out of black cotton material just so I could blend into the shadows if required. I believe now to be just such an occasion. Now if you could draw your attention away from legs we might make more progress towards our escape. Please lead on."

"Please Polly, I would be much happier if you took the lead, the view would be far more pleasant."

"Do you want me to change you into a frog, because I can you know?"

Innocent smirked at her but turned and made his way over to a small set of stairs leading up to an opening, covered with a hatch.

"Douse your light, I think we should work to remain in the shadows, if we are in luck they haven't secured it, thinking us well constrained and unable to get this far," he said.

He carefully went up the stairs and placed his hands on the hatch. Pushing it he whispered, "mistake number two I think." He raised the hatch a tiny amount and brought himself up so that he could look through the gap he had made.

"All seems quiet, wait here," he said as he pushed the hatch up a little more and squeezed through and was gone.

Polly stood at the bottom of the stairs listening for any sign that Innocent's escape had been noticed but in moments the hatch was opened fully and he reached down a hand to help her up and out.

"Mistake number three, they are all sheltering inside the main cabin away from the cold. There isn't anyone on lookout."

"We're not doing the counting game again are we?" said Polly as she stood next to him and looked around. They were at the back of the deck, in the shadows made by the cabins and deck above them. Across the deck she could see candle light flickering in the main cabins and the silhouettes of men sitting around a table.

"I like the counting game, Col never complains."

"Hmm," said Polly.

"Come on," said Innocent, "we are at the right end, nearest the shore. There's a ladder over there we can climb down and be on solid ground before you know it."

He bent down to bring himself below the level of the edges of the wooden railings along the side of the ship and carefully led her over to the ladder leading down to a wooden jetty that jutted out from the main pier area. Innocent began to stand up so that he could step over and onto it but then stopped.

"What is it?" asked Polly.

"A thought just occurred to me. What if our escape from the hold wasn't meant to be that difficult? Maybe there are men waiting on shore to see if we do escape and they might be more attentive. If they are more attentive then this is the spot they would focus on."

"It's certainly a possibility, it does seem a little stupid of them all to be in the Captain's cabin and easily seen by us."

"Consider it this way as well, if they thought we couldn't escape, well great we don't and they get rid of us out at sea. But hey maybe we do escape. If I'm shot whilst climbing a ladder, who is to say I was going up or down the said ladder? All they have to claim is that they thought I was someone who was doing something nefarious. Admittedly your friend, Quinn might not buy their story but that would be little consolation to me if we were dead."

"Nor would that please me much either, now that I am added to your narrative. Can you see anything?"

Innocent carefully raised his head so that he could look over the wooden railing.

"No, just a dark quay but let's wait a bit."

Carefully they both studied the dark quayside ahead of them. Then Innocent whispered.

"Over there to the right, I just saw the tip of a cigarette glow behind that stack of bales."

"You were right then, very well not that way then. Perhaps we could work our way round them. If we went over the other side into the water, we could swim to the shore and climb up another jetty and surprise them."

"We could but for one small problem."

"What's that?"

"I can't swim."

Polly sighed in exasperation. "Really! You don't half make things complicated. Very well then, magic it is but you will need to carry me if I get too tired."

"Get us past those men and I will gladly carry you all the way back to the Inn. Any chance you could fly us over them?"

"Don't be ridiculous Innocent."

"Just thought it might be fun, I've never flown anywhere before. So what is your plan?"

"Already happening Inno, look at the sea, there is a mist rolling in, soon they won't be able to see their hands in front of their face, let alone us climbing down a ladder."

"If they can't see, doesn't the same hold true for us? How are we going to see?"

"When we get to the bottom of the ladder, hold on to my hand, I will get us out."

"Won't they hear our footsteps as we go past them?"

"So many questions. Let me ask one in return, have you ever tried to sneak a werewolf back into an orphanage after lights out?"

"Can't say I have."

"Then do not question my ability now. Don't worry, the mist will hide us and I will muffle the sound of our footsteps."

"You are a very useful girl to know but I'm guessing you already know that."

"Will has pointed it out on numerous occasions."

"Can I ask, just in case we don't survive the night? Just so I know, you and he aren't"

"Aren't what Inno?"

"You know."

"No, I don't know, now sh, it won't matter how much I muffle the sound of our footsteps if they hear you speaking."

"You are also very annoying," said Innocent.

Polly just grinned at him and as the mist thickened around them she pushed him towards the rope ladder. With a sigh he swung himself over the rail and disappeared into the deepening mist. Polly followed him immediately and once her feet touched the wood decking, she reached out and grabbed hold of Innocent's hand.

She concentrated on the mist in front of her and then whispered the spell that would allow only her to see through it. As she had half explained to Innocent this had been almost the first combination spell she had ever managed to hold on to. Sneaking Will back into the orphanage when he had been in wolf form had proved more and more difficult until she had worked out how to make a mist form to hide them both. Then she worked out the spell that allowed her to walk through it as though it wasn't there, whilst also muffling the sound of their footsteps. Now she was very grateful for that early challenge as she led Innocent up onto the main quay and along its length toward freedom. She could hear the hidden men whispering amongst themselves.

"Can you see any fink?"

"Not a thing but don't worry they won't 'ave made it off the ship."

"But what if they do?"

"Then we would 'ear them wouldn't we. You know how this quay creaks; no one would be able to sneak past us."

"He's right, don't anyone move a muscle. That way if we hear anything we fire, bound to catch 'em then," said a third man.

Polly felt Innocent's hand tighten in hers and she could feel his anger radiate through their link. She squeezed his hand in support and led him past the waiting men. She wondered just who Innocent had upset because the ambush was three rows deep. Just as she began to feel they were safe, she saw further men crouched behind bales of hay and crates full of produce ready to be loaded onto waiting ships.

Only when they had reached the safety of a street beyond the dockside did she let go and turn to hug him. Innocent hugged her back in appreciation. When she pulled away he took her hand and kissed it gently.

"You are a blooming marvel woman. You are seriously stacking up the debt I owe you," he whispered.

"Don't think about it Innocent, we all have our skills, I'm sure you would have come up with a solution if you needed one."

"Yes but it would have been a bloody mess and I might not have survived. This way is much cleaner and better for my soul."

"I still think we should be careful on our way back we don't know what awaits us."

"We need to be careful indeed. Unless you've forgotten, because I certainly haven't, you are wandering around in a state of undress. I'm not sure my reputation will survive if I'm seen wandering around this fair city with a woman in her bloomers. Highly scandalous."

Polly laughed, "So the idea of assassins in the dark holds few fears for you but being seen with me like this gives you palpitations."

"In more ways than you can imagine my dear," Innocent said with a raised eyebrow.

"Then I will show you what anyone walking past us will see."

She clicked her fingers and laughed to see Innocent's look of amazement. She knew she looked perfect, the illusion she used showed that her hair was well styled, piled high on her head with little curls falling alongside her face. Her corset was immaculate and her skirt was back in place.

"Very clever my dear, though I have to admit I prefer the real you."

Polly laughed, clicked her fingers again and was back to having her hair all messy and nothing below her corset but her bloomers, tights and boots which were now in real need of a clean. Innocent took a hanky out of his jacket pocket and leant down to wipe what must have been a smudge of dirt from her forehead.

"There, perfect again, the most beautiful woman in London," he smiled and Polly felt a tingle go through her at his attention.

"Flattery will get you nowhere Mr Innocent," she said, "Now how do we get into the Inn without being seen, if it is under siege?"

"There is an entrance to the Inn which I have ensured is known only to those I trust. It is a street away from the square so I fully expect us to be able to enter it without being seen. We shall tread carefully even though they will not be expecting us to get to them as soon as we will."

He took hold of her hand again and they walked away from the quayside and back into the dark London streets.

###

Will wiped sweat and gunpowder residue from his face. He was tired from continually looking outside but behind him he could tell that Rachel had a musket and pistol loaded and ready for him.

"Can you see anything" she whispered.

"They 'ain't moving from their spots, all nice and secure. They're being too canny to leave themselves open for a shot to get through to 'em. 'ighly annoying if you ask me. I got to keep firing to make 'em wary of coming out into the open. We've hit a stalemate."

"I guess they are 'oping we run out of ammunition before they do. Perhaps we could tempt them out, make 'em think we 'ave run out of ammunition and then pick a few off when they attack."

"You're a blood thirsty little thing ain't you," said Will smiling.

"I'm just getting tired; it's been a long night."

"That it 'as, look come down 'ere near my feet, I don't reckon a bullet would hit you there, if you bring one of the cushions over from the bench you could sleep for a bit. I can keep watch."

"No, I won't sleep, I'm not leaving you alone, I just want something to 'appen, either good or bad, that way the night will be over."

"No use thinking about such things, instead tell me about your family, you got anyone special? You going to be doing anything nice for Christmas?"

"I'll be 'ere for Christmas, you ought to see the spread Mr Innocent puts out for us, you've never seen so much food."

"What does 'e serve then?"

"Roast beef, goose, vegetable dishes that are full of cream and spices, wine better than any we normally serve here, it's a veritable feast I tell you, I bet the Queen don't 'ave a better dinner."

"I bet you 'ave more fun as well, a day off from working."

"We laugh all day, Mr Innocent treat us like royalty 'e don't make us lift a finger to do anything. It's proper magical it is."

Jane came in to the room and looked across at Will.

"Col wants to know how it's going in here," she said.

"Nothing much is 'appening, they can't get to us and we can't get to them. I'm conserving me ammunition."

"It's the same out the front, Col's wondering if we should do something to get them to attack."

"We are still outnumbered. We was just talking about something like that 'ere as well but I think the odds are still against us. We 'aven't been able to pick any of 'em off yet and if they get in 'ere we are outnumbered at least two to one and I don't fancy our chances against 'em."

"I'll tell him we wait then and keep going as we are."

"Something will break, we 'aven't 'eard from Innocent or Polly yet and I'm betting on 'em getting back 'ere before first light."

"You believe they are alive then, we aren't defending this place for someone who is dead and gone?"

"Polly's got more tricks up 'er sleeve than any magician you could name and trust me I would know if she was dead. I would 'ave felt it. They'll come back I promise."

"Will look, there's a light flashing behind 'em, do you think it is Innocent and Polly?" Rachel said looking out of the window.

Will came up to her and looked out. The light flashed again and he smiled.

"It's not Polly, that's Gadget and I 'ope she's got a good plan."

"She's just a kid, what can she do."

"You'd be surprised; she plays on that, being just a kid. Kids get ignored don't they, they just 'ang around, nobody pays 'em any attention. I wonder what she's up too, it'll be something downright sneaky knowing 'er. Jane go back to Col and tell 'im to 'ang on, if Gadget is back that means something is going to turn up, she's 'ighly resourceful."

Jane turned around and ran back out to the main part of the inn.

"See if you can catch sight of any kids but don't call attention to 'em if you do, just let me know."

"Something's happening Will, look behind that wagon, what's that light?"

"Bloody 'ell, that's dynamite. Gadget get out of there, I can't fire until I know you aren't there."

Will lifted his musket, sighted and waited as he saw a man rise and begin to creep around the wagon. He swore.

"Jesus, where are you Gadget, I daren't fire too soon."

"I see a light way behind 'em, it's flickering like before, Gadget's out of the way," said Rachel.

Will fired, the man jerked and dropped the stick of dynamite and it sputtered on the ground, the fuse still burning. Another man came running out to pick it up but Rachel took the musket from Will and handed him another immediately. He raised the musket up and fired before the man could do more than reach for the dynamite. The man fell over just as the dynamite blew up, his body disintegrating as the explosion ripped through him. The blast ripped through the wagons and men screamed as they were hit by the wood flying straight towards them.

"Quick Rachel load the musket, they will be coming now."

Rachel shuddered at the sight of bits of body that lay scattered over the ground but quickly passed Will another loaded musket and began loading more as she shouted to Jane to come and help.

Jane ran through the door, picked up a musket and loaded it as Will aimed at the men emerging from behind the destroyed wagons. Will fired, passed the musket back, another was placed in his hand and he raised it up to fire again. Then he passed that one back and received another. He kept firing and it felt like time had stopped and all that he could do was fire, take another musket and fire again. He was aware at one point that someone was firing next to him, but he couldn't spare the time to look to see which of the women it was. Then as suddenly as the attack had started the attackers fell back and no more men ran towards them. All that was left on the ground in front of the inn were the bodies of those that had died in their attempt to reach the defenders. The echoes of gun fire faded away and silence fell.

Will put down the musket in his hands with relief and looked across at Rachel as she stared at the scene outside the inn with horror on her face.

"My God", said Rachel, "they're dead, all of them, we killed 'em all."

Will reached across and took the musket out of her trembling hands and leant it against the wall. She reached out to him and he hugged her gently as she shook in reaction to what she had done.

"They would have killed us Rachel; we could not have done anything different, unless we wished to die ourselves."

Rachel stepped back and looked up at him.

"I know," she said gently.

Will looked around and saw that Jane and Tilly were both stood nearby with loaded muskets in their hands.

Will took one from Jane.

"Tilly, give that musket to Rachel. We have broken this attack but they may try something else. Jane go back to Col, tell him to watch out, they will be getting desperate, Tilly go with her. Rachel and I will stay here."

Jane stared at Will for a moment then nodded, turned and left with Tilly close behind her

4 DAWN

Innocent and Polly heard the explosion just as they came to the edge of Soho.

"Bloody hell, I hope that hasn't hit the Inn, it won't survive a blast like that."

"Let's keep our hopes up Innocent, there is no cheer of victory sounding. But I think it would be good if we could get into the Inn as soon as possible, that way we can help the fight."

"Come this way, there is a tunnel entrance through one of my buildings."

He led her down a quiet alley and was about to go to a door when it was flung open and Gadget came running out.

"Polly, Polly, you are safe, thank goodness, we were so worried," Gadget threw herself onto Polly and hugged her as tightly as she could.

Polly held on for a moment but then pulled away and looked down at Gadget.

"What's been happening Gadget?" she asked.

"These men came to take over the Inn earlier but Will 'eard them in time, so Col sorted everyone out to defend it and sent me out to get 'elp. He said to go for Quinn but I 'ad a better idea."

"Really and what was your idea? Surely the law would have been a good solution."

"Nah, my idea was much better and I was just going back into the Inn to tell Col that it would be alright now. Though I 'ave to admit to just sending two of my crew to get Quinn just like Will asked."

"I think we should keep moving Polly, I want to get into the tunnel and into my Inn before anybody round here learns of my successful escape," said Innocent.

"Of course, please Innocent lead the way."

Innocent opened the door and turned to Polly, "Shall we, I am eager to see my friend again."

Polly followed him inside and Gadget came in behind her, shutting the door before she struck a match and lit the lantern she had in her hand.

Innocent led them through the house, down into the cellar and across to a blank part of the wall. He pulled on a lamp fitting and with a smooth glide a door opened and he motioned for them to enter.

Once inside he reached up for a lever and the door slid silently closed.

"So now Gadget you can answer, what was the explosion? Is the Inn still standing?"

"Yes, it was a close thing though, I was round the back and I signalled to Will I was back and doing something, then I could see 'em with the dynamite, I knew that Will wouldn't do anything if he thought I was in danger so I grabbed all me crew and we ran for it, got out of range, signalled back to Will and then all hell broke free. I reckon as how Will got the man with the stick of dynamite and he was too close to the wagon with the rest of it in and so the whole thing blew up. Those men not killed by the wagons blowing up began to run towards the Inn but Will and someone else just kept firing, I don't know how they managed to do it so quickly but none of 'em got anywhere close. I came running back round 'ere to see 'ow the rest of me crew were doing and I got two of 'em to go and get Quinn and the rest to take what they 'ad along the tunnel. I was just about to shut the door and follow 'em when I saw you."

"What had your crew got Gadget?" said Polly.

"I'll show you when we get back in but don't worry Polly, it's all over now, whoever they are they've failed."

"You seem very certain of yourself young lady," said Innocent.

"I am," she said smiling and hugging her satchel to herself.

"Very well, we can wait for your information but let's get into the Inn so that we can see how things are faring," said Innocent. He picked up the speed and soon they saw light filtering along the dark corridor. They came around a corner and there in front of them was an open door leading into the cellars of The Hangman's Dance. A young boy was stood there holding the door and his anxious look disappeared as he saw Gadget. She called out to him.

"Toby, didn't I tell you to shut the door behind you?"

His face crumpled in apology.

"I'm, I'm sorry Gadget but you said you's was right behind me so I thought I'd wait for you."

"You'd 'ave been in a right state if we'd got killed and it was the enemy running towards you."

"Leave the boy alone Gadget," said Polly "we didn't get killed so no harm done. It took years before Will would do as I ask so give the boy time to learn."

The boy grinned up at her and then ran across the cellar and up the stairs shouting as he went. "They're 'ere, Mr Col, they're back just like you said they'd be."

"I hope no-one on the outside can hear him, otherwise our element of surprise is going to be totally ruined," said Innocent dryly. "Shall we go and find out what has been happening here?"

He went over to the stairs and Polly and Gadget followed closely behind him. The smell of gunpowder hit Polly as she came into the main room. Col was stood near an open window looking out into the square, he turned and smiled at them.

"I knew you'd be back. Will told me that Polly would get you both home."

"And you believed that Polly would get me here rather than refuting him and saying that I would be able to rescue myself? I'm beginning to lose my sneaky reputation, it is becoming most irksome."

Col laughed, "I knew the two of you were more than a match for some guttersnipes who thought they could get the better of you."

Innocent went over to him, touched him on the shoulder and carefully looked out of the window. "Now let's see who has the temerity to attack my home."

Polly looked at Gadget who was jumping up and down in excitement.

"Alright Gadget, tell me what you and your crew have collected?"

"All their spare ammunition Polly. Now all they've got left is what is in their pouches. And we managed to get most of their powder wet. They is soon going to realise they ain't got no bullets and no way to fire nothing else at us even if they did."

Polly was about to say something about double negatives when Will came running in from the other room. He swept her up into a hug and spun her around.

"I knew you was safe, I knew it but damn it, it's good to 'ave you back Polly."

"It's good to be back Will, now please put me down, I don't believe the evening's entertainment is over quite yet."

"They're done out back, ain't nobody moving. Rachel is keeping watch and a couple of Gadget's friends are with her. So I reckon we're safe from attack from that direction for a bit."

Polly went over to Innocent and looked out into the square. The men out there were still hidden behind the overturned wagons and bales.

"Have they done anything Col since the explosion? We heard it at the outskirts of Soho, they must know something has happened," she said.

"They haven't moved Polly; I don't think the severity of the situation has quite hit them yet."

"Look, one of them is coming out," said Maeve looking through the other window.

The man had stood up with his hands up in the air to show he wasn't carrying any weapon. He stepped out in front of the wagons and smiled.

"It seems you have managed to defeat some of my men but do not believe the night is over. You are still outnumbered and your boss is dead. Give up this fight and let us come in. I am still prepared to discuss the possibility of your continuing existence."

Innocent gave a small sigh.

"Big Jed McCafferty, of course, I should have realised it was him attempting a take-over when we ended up in the hold of a stinking ship."

"Who is he?" asked Polly.

"He owns all the bars along the roughest part of the docks. There's not a rape, mugging or press ganging that isn't done without his knowledge along that stretch. He's not likely to want to give up even if he knows he can't win. He's never known what it is to lose."

"What's in the street behind him?" said Maeve, "there's a flashing light."

"That's morse code," said Col. "Give me a moment and I'll . . . . bloody hell, it's Quinn. He's got here."

"My turn then I think," said Innocent and he moved into view.

"Hello Big Jed," he called out and laughed as the man swore.

"Before you do anything rash I feel obliged to point out that you are surrounded by the law. My good friend, Detective Quinn, has brought a few of his colleagues to round you up. You should also check your ammunition levels as I believe you will find them a little depleted."

Big Jed turned and looked behind him. His men were rushing around behind the wagons and shouts of annoyance rose into the night air. Then one of the men swore and ran into the dark streets. His actions galvanised the rest of the attackers, as like rats leaving a sinking ship, the rest followed him. From the sounds of men being hit and the whistles of the policemen ringing around the square it was obvious that none of them got very far. Soon those that had run were being escorted back into the square, handcuffed and held by burly constables.

Innocent went to the front door of the Inn and opened it.

"Your take-over bid doesn't seem to have been too successful my dear fellow. I suggest you surrender and accept your fate."

Big Jed looked around at his men and his shoulders slumped.

"Seems you've won Innocent but don't think your reign will last much longer, too many of us think you're getting soft. Keep your eyes on the darkness, we'll be there waiting for you to slip up." He turned and began to hold his arms out as if expecting a constable to step forward to handcuff him. Innocent looked back at the Inn and smiled.

Suddenly a shot rang out and Innocent fell to the floor. Polly screamed and ran out to him. Before she could get to him, he was picking himself up and brushing dirt from his trousers.

Polly stopped and stared as Quinn came into the square carrying a smoking pistol and stood next to Big Jed's body. He turned him over and Polly could see a pistol held in his right hand.

"I saw him draw the pistol from his coat as he turned and admit I was half tempted to let him kill you Innocent but I decided I preferred the devil I knew above the one I didn't." Quinn smiled at Innocent.

Innocent shivered. "I am in your debt Sir."

Quinn smiled again, "The dawn is approaching and it seems you have had another eventful night. I will need to take down the particulars of the attack upon your place of business but if you can give me the basics I can wait for your full statement."

"Please come inside Quinn. I will get some coffee prepared and we can tell you what we've been through."

"I will get my men organised and a wagon righted so that the body can be taken back to the morgue, then I will join you." He looked at Polly and grinned "nice to see you Polly, though I would advise you to find some more clothing before running out into public again."

Polly laughed and curtsied, "I hope I have not shocked you Quinn, I will go and borrow a skirt, circumstances meant I had to lose my original one."

Quinn smiled, bowed and went over to his men to organise taking the prisoners to the police station and the corpse to the morgue.

Innocent looked at Polly. "I believe you do care about me, the way you came running to my aid."

"I was simply annoyed that after working so hard to get you back here you were felled by a cheap trick."

"Keep telling yourself that Polly, I will hold onto the truth I believe," he said smiling down at her.

He took her hand and they went back into the inn.

"One thing I am curious about," Innocent said as they came back into the main room, "how did Big Jed know that the Inn was going to be empty last night."

Maeve stepped forward, tears running down her face. "I'm so sorry Mr Innocent; I think it was my fault."

"Why?" said Innocent.

"This dock worker 'ad become a regular over the last month, spent loads on me, kept asking for more visits. Then I told 'im I wasn't free tonight and 'e kept on and on badgering me to see 'im. In the end I told 'im it was because the Inn was shut. It was my fault Innocent, I'm so, so sorry."

Innocent went over to her and gently hugged her.

"Please Maeve, don't be upset, you didn't mean to cause any problems. I'm far happier knowing that you were tricked into giving away the information than discovering a rat within my operation."

"But I did you wrong Mr Innocent."

"No you didn't Maeve and I hold no anger for your actions at all. Please do not distress yourself. Look we are all here, no-one has been harmed. There are a few more bullet holes in the décor but that will just add to its charm."

"But there must be something I can do to make up for my mistake."

"In actual fact there is Maeve. Polly needs a skirt; if you have a spare she could borrow I'm sure she would be most grateful."

Maeve looked over at Polly and smiled. "Gladly Mr Innocent, I will go and find 'er something nice." She ran over to the stairs and disappeared from view.

Col looked at Innocent. "Nicely done Inno."

"What good would it do being angry when no harm was intended. Poor girl she will blame herself enough without me adding to it."

Innocent looked around and saw the other girls standing there. "Though her being here begs the question. Col why are the girls here?"

"They wouldn't leave Inno and I don't think we'd have held out so successfully without them."

Innocent looked over them and Polly could see their loyalty to him meant a great deal. He went to speak, dipped his head for a moment and then looked up at all of them with a gentle smile on his face and Polly would have sworn tears in his eyes.

"Then you all have my gratitude and be assured I will reward you appropriately." Innocent blinked and nodded his head once. "Now I think it is time we all relaxed. Gadget, is there one of your crew I can trust with some money. I believe that breakfast needs to be delivered."

"I'll go myself Mr Innocent," said Gadget, "I know the best shops to go to and then you can pay 'em when they deliver. They'll do that for me." Before Innocent could say anything further she was gone.

"Does she ever slow down?" he asked Polly as he collapsed into one of his larger sofas and sighed with relief.

"Hardly ever," Polly said sitting down beside him.

Innocent looked around at everyone. "Come all, sit down relax, let's do nothing whilst we wait for breakfast to arrive, stories can be told when Quinn gets here. That way we won't have to say things twice. I know I for one could do with forty winks."

He leant back into the sofa and closed his eyes. The others in the room followed suit and soon a comfortable silence fell over the room that had been filled with the noise of battle all night. The takeover bid had failed.

ABOUT THE AUTHOR

Samantha Parry lives in London and is normally to be found sitting in an office coping with the daily grind. But away from that she holds to her self-made childhood promise to never reach the age of not believing and her imagination provides her with lots of crimes for her intrepid duo, Baker & Dagger to investigate. Her first story for Baker & Dagger was initially published by Antimatter Press in their Anthology of New Writing published in 2015.
Now that story introduces this first book of five novelettes about Pollyanne Baker and William Dagger.

22316963R00097

Printed in Great Britain
by Amazon